Dear Reader,

I grew up in New York City, and according to my birth certificate, I was born there, but I've come to the conclusion that my records must have been falsified. As soon as I took my first walk through the pristine, pine-scented woods in northern Minnesota, I felt as if I had come home, completely at peace with myself and everything around me. Without the distractions of the city, I was able to concentrate on my music. Inspired by my beautiful surroundings, the melodies flowed so quickly I could barely get them down on paper fast enough.

But nature's beauty wasn't the only thing in Minnesota that staked its claim on my soul and brought me an inner peace that I'd never experienced before. I found a special lady there, my winter lady, the woman who thawed through my defenses and warmed my frozen heart.

Devlin Paige

Minnesota

MEN MADE IN AMERICA

JANET JOYCE
Winter Lady

Minnesota

Silhouette® Books

Published by Silhouette Books New York

America's Publisher of Contemporary Romance

Dedicated to the two men
who have warmed our lives for many winters—
J. and J.

SILHOUETTE BOOKS
300 East 42nd St., New York, N.Y. 10017

WINTER LADY

Copyright © 1983 by Janet Joyce

ISBN: 0-373-45173-3

Published Silhouette Books 1983, 1993

All the characters in this book have no existence outside the imagination of the author and have no relation whatsoever to anyone bearing the same name or names. They are not even distantly inspired by any individual known or unknown to the author, and all incidents are pure invention.

® and ™ are trademarks used under license. Trademarks recorded with ® are registered in the United States Patent and Trademark Office, the Canadian Trade Marks Office and in other countries.

Printed in the U.S.A.

One

Raine Morgan spiked the tips of her ski poles into the crusty ice at the top of the hill and lifted her dark goggles away from her large brown eyes. White swirling snow and stinging cold needles lashed her cheeks and clung to the thick wool of her knickers and heavy socks. The desolate hills of northern Minnesota seemed to close in on her as she tried to get her bearings. Everywhere she looked the land-scape appeared the same—stark, frozen and thick with snow-laden firs.

There was no doubt about it—she had no idea where she was and the rising wind was making it almost impossible to see more than a few feet in front of her. She had been warned that a storm was brewing, but having lived all her life in Minnesota, she didn't fear a coming snowfall. Now, she berated herself for making the pompous assumption that one snowstorm was the same as another. She had grown complacent living in Minneapolis, where the streets were cleared off before the snow stopped and the buildings sheltered people from the frigid wind. In the city, she had never been afraid. Up north, however, standing alone in a bleak pine forest listening to the whistling wind pick up and slice through the trees was a different story.

She should have returned to the Piney Edge Lodge long ago, but somehow she had lost her way on the path laid out for cross-country skiers. With every shush of her skies she went farther and farther into the mammoth pine forest. This was a very bad start to her week's vacation from her job at *Today's Woman* magazine.

She had planned to take advantage of the cross-country skiing offered at the winter resort. Raine replaced her goggles and began a slow snowplow down the steep incline, gasping as her skis slid on the iced terrain and her speed increased. She had thought herself a proficient skier, but it was becoming painfully obvious to her that the pleasant inclines of Lowry Park in Minneapolis were nothing compared with the steep rock-strewn hills of northern Minnesota.

The wind howled through the trees—a lonely, eerie sound that sent shivers up Raine's spine. The biting cold was rapidly numbing her cheeks and creeping beneath her green woolen tousle cap to nip at her ears. She had to find some kind of shelter—and soon! Panting and exhausted by the time she had maneuvered herself down to the bottom of the hill, she stood silently, fighting for breath, knowing she had to stay in control.

She was in a ravine, with steep cliffs on both sides and large granite boulders strewn along the narrow treeless clearing. She heard a gurgling noise and looked down. Paralyzed by horror and fear, she realized that she was balanced on ice and it was slowly crackling in a line away from her and toward a dark hole of moving water. What she had mistaken for the floor of a small valley was in reality the bed of a frozen river. Without knowing it, she had begun skiing across the snow-covered ice. Hearing the noise of the water as it relentlessly ate away at the thin ice, Raine knew she had to act quickly but was too terrified to think straight.

Did she dare move forward and take the chance of breaking through the ice and drowning before she reached the opposite shore, or should she attempt to go back the way she came? She thought she heard something moving in the shadows of the cliffs above the riverbank and shuddered. She was sure something was up there, watching her—some animal prepared to attack! Every tale she had heard about the wild animals who inhabited the north woods flashed through her mind. Frantically she searched the long shadows overhead and when one seemed to move, she panicked. Her scream shattered the silence and she backed away without thinking, dread hastening her jerky movements.

The ice split beneath her and before she could twist away, she was plunged into the freezing water. Pain shot through her shocked system as she sank like lead in her heavy clothes. She struggled to get out of her skis, but knew as she felt her booted feet break free of the bindings that she was going to die. She took a last gasping breath and the dark cold water closed over her head. Raine struggled beneath the surface, hampered by her sodden clothes. Her lungs were on fire, bursting inside her, but she could not take a breath. She had to fight, had to live, but the water was an enemy without mercy. She felt a tension at the back of her neck, and uselessly her hands clawed at the constricting pull that was choking her even as her body screamed for one last breath. Her will to fight dissipated beneath the frigid black water that claimed her, and she opened her mouth.

It was cold, so cold. Raine was in a void without light, without sound, only pain. "Breathe, damn you!" The harsh curse came from far away, but there was nothing she could do as a sharp painful pressure shoved water from her lungs and she coughed and retched. Her struggles were weak, useless, and she let herself be pounded and pummeled like a lifeless rag doll. Who was hurting her? Who was slapping her face and covering her blue lips with fire? Oxygen filled her lungs; then someone lifted and held her around the waist. Cut in half by a length of steel, she dangled head-down until ice water ran out of her mouth and crisp cold air rushed back into her lungs. She whimpered like a half-drowned kitten as violent shivers wracked her body. Tears were frozen on her cheeks, but she had no strength to brush them away. She was being wrapped in something thick and heavy, lifted over a broad shoulder, and she could do nothing but shake with a cold so deep it cut to the bone.

"We're almost there," the deep voice of her rescuer promised, but she was only conscious of the need to keep her eyes closed and escape the terrible cold that gripped her body.

She was dreaming. It was a warm summer's day and she and Darryl had gone to the beach. She spread a blanket out on the warm sand and lay down on her back, feeling the warmth of the July sun toast her arms and legs. A shiver raised goose flesh on her skin as a cool breeze came across the lake and swept the shore. She rolled onto her side and heard Darryl's voice by her ear. "Hold still." She smiled at him, happily nestling against his chest until the wind was gone and she was warm again. She felt his hand on the fastening of her bikini and slapped it away, but he continued to undress her despite her protests. His hands were warm and gentle and his voice tenderly persuasive.

His image wavered and became that of Bob Williams, her former fiancé. "I love you, but I want a career," she whispered, telling Bob that she could not marry him if he forbade her to go on to college and then work.

Half in and half out of her dream world, her mind rambled. She remembered the day she had left for college. Bob had tried again to persuade her to stay and marry him, but she had turned him down. "No, Bob...I'm sorry," she murmured, and climbed into the back seat of her parents' car. He had stood in the graveled drive, watching her until the family car drove out of sight.

Four and one-half years later, she had taken her first job as girl Friday on the staff of *Today's Woman*. At twenty-five, she now held the hard-earned position of associate editor. Her assignments, to date, were centered in the food department. She hoped to transfer to the current events department as soon as the senior editor considered her experienced enough to hold the more demanding position. Darryl

Standish was one of the magazine's photographers, and they had dated occasionally during the past year.

Suddenly, Raine felt terribly warm, smothered by the hot blankets that had somehow slipped over her. She struggled up out of the constricting covers, intending to tell Darryl that she was too hot, that she didn't need blankets on top of her on such a warm day.

She opened her eyes, not to the sun or the beach, but to a gray-lit room and the sound of a howling winter wind. She was in a strange room, a room that she had never seen before. The walls were of rough-hewn pine, and a large stone fireplace stood against one of them. The fire was low, casting long shadows across the planked hardwood floor toward the bed where she was lying. She looked down at the coarse homespun quilt that covered her lower limbs, startled when she realized she had nothing on beneath the blanket. Frantically, she pulled the quilt up over her breasts as her eyes searched the small cabin. In the weak light coming from the window, she could see shapes draped across a line by the fireplace. As her eyes adjusted to the contrasting shadows beyond the bed, she recognized that it was her clothing hanging on the line.

How had she gotten here? Who had stripped her of her clothing? Visions of herself slipping beneath the black water of the ice-covered river came back, and she gasped as awareness of all that had transpired returned.

"Breathe, damn you!" The terse order rang clear inside her head, and she willed herself to remain calm. Sensing a presence, Raine slowly turned her head and found a sleeping masculine figure on the other side of the large framed bed. Shock held her rigid as her eyes traveled the expanse of bare, golden brown muscled flesh across the broad chest, traced a line up from the strong neck to the sculptured features of a ruggedly handsome face. Unruly dark auburn hair was cut long over a tanned forehead. His cheeks were bronzed, his nose, patrician, straight above a molded mouth that drooped slightly open in sleep. His lower lip had a sensuous fullness that looked curiously vulnerable. His chin jutted stubbornly, burrowed into the white down-filled pillow pulled close to his face. One arm was thrown over his head, the other hidden beneath the quilt. As Raine stared at him in stupefied disbelief, his long lashes lifted and she found herself gazing into a pair of deep hazel eyes with dangerous gold flecks. He seemed oddly familiar, but he had to be a stranger. She was alone in a cabin, stark naked, with a man lying peacefully beside her in the same natural state!

"Good morning," he said cheerfully, bringing both arms behind his head as he propped himself up on the pillow. His eyes dropped meaningfully to her breasts, where the quilt had slipped down. His all-seeing gaze broke through her paralysis of shock and she snatched at the fallen covering, dragging it, this time, up beneath her chin, as he smiled with amusement.

"You are even more enticing to look at in the morning than you are at night." He ignored the furious blush burning in her cheeks and rolled off the bed. By the time he had pulled on a pair of faded blue denims, she had her eyes tightly closed, totally mortified. She heard his dry laugh as he walked to the bathroom, and she opened her eyes as he disappeared through the doorway, carrying a sweater and a pair of leather boots.

"Do you have a name?" he called conversationally from behind the closed door, but

Raine was still too stunned to answer. He had a magnificent physique, his naked body tanned a deep brown all over. He didn't get that tan in the winter sun of northern Minnesota, and she wondered who on earth he was. She knew immediately what his thoughts about her were. His hazel eyes had glinted a warm sherry brown as they traveled across her. She could still feel the heat of his gaze and shivered in reaction. His mating call inspired an instinctive response deep inside her, and she was shocked by the strength of it. She would have to be very careful with this man and his drugging aura of virility.

She nervously brushed back a long strand of topaz blond hair that had fallen across her eyes, and stared at the door to the bathroom, unable to move. What did one say to a strange man when one found oneself naked in his bed? The door opened and he was back in the room, fully dressed. He strode from window to window, pulling open the short tab-topped curtains to allow the pale morning light to filter through the frost-coated panes. "Still snowing," he said, and without looking at her crossed the room to a large, wood-burning cookstove.

"Perhaps a cup of coffee will loosen your tongue." He pumped water from a small painted pump at the side of a freestanding sink into a blue-spattered enamel pot. Setting it to one side, he pushed rolled paper into the grate of the large, black iron stove and lit a match on the heel of his boot. He threw the lit tinder into the stove and pulled an iron cover over the opening. Measuring coffee into the pot, he placed it on the stove. When he was done with that chore, he dragged an oak chair across the wooden floor and straddled it. He rested his arms across the back of the chair and looked at her. "Now, pretty girl, perhaps you'll tell me why you were standing in the middle of a half-frozen river with water closing over your charming blond head?"

"I was skiing," she said, stupidly, and when her remark brought a quirk to his lips, she felt her temper rise. Her lips tightened mutinously. She had a few questions of her own.

"Who are you?" she managed, feeling at a distinct disadvantage, her skin burning beneath the quilt. It seemed he wanted her to be aware of her precarious position, for his gaze probed the edges of the heavy blanket whenever she breathed. Her sharp question, which had a decidedly hysterical edge to it, appeared to annoy him.

"Come, now, Miss whoever-you-are. My identity is not in question. It's yours I'm worried about. How did you discover where I'm staying?"

Her brows drew together in confusion. Hadn't he carried her here? Had someone else rescued her from the water and brought her to his cabin? No, he knew about her horrible experience in the river. "Didn't you bring me?" She looked at his narrowed, sharp gaze and sat straighter in the bed, firmly retaining her grip on the quilt. "Now look, mister. If you'll give me my clothes, I'll be on my way. I want to thank you very much for rescuing me.... You saved my life... and...." She looked down at herself, thinking about the lengths he had taken to treat her for hypothermia. She was remembering everything a little bit clearer the longer she was awake. She recalled her dream and knew that her mind had tried to escape the clinging cold of her shivering body with thoughts of a sun-swept beach. She remembered the voice in her dream. It hadn't been Darryl's voice at all, but this man's, telling her to hold still, telling her to relax and let his body warm her. She had followed his instructions meekly, felt his bare flesh heating her icy skin and had tried to erase the intimacy by pretending it was all part of a dream. "And... thank you for everything you did last night."

"Ahh..." He grinned in quick understanding. "So, I wasn't Darryl or Bob all of the time. You were aware of being held by someone else?" He spoke insolently, as if she had lessened herself in his eyes by escaping to a dream world when reality had been so terrifying.

"I...I knew some of the time," she admitted, holding up her chin defiantly. "You were very kind, but now I must get back to the lodge. Do you have a phone?"

"No!" he snapped. "We are quite isolated here. No phone, no car and no easy way out until this weather clears."

"But people will be worried about me," she exclaimed. "I have to notify the lodge that I'm safe."

"Your *friends* will just have to worry," he snarled sarcastically. "Look outside. We're trapped here." His voice grew steadily louder as he glared at her. "The nearest resort is almost ten miles away. I watched your rather disjointed method of slithering down that hill yesterday. You could never have skied this far. You were trying to get to this exact destination, but whoever dropped you off on the road didn't know that you'd ski over the first hill and into a river.''

"No one dropped me here! I got lost." She didn't realize that her large brown eyes reflected a rueful expression that made her look like a guileless child. ''I promise to pay more attention to the markers next time. Isn't there some way I can get back to Piney Edge?'' Perhaps the humility in her voice would breach the stern and frightening expression on his face. He must not have enjoyed rescuing her any better than she had enjoyed being subject to the most terrifying ordeal she had ever been through. She steadfastly refused to think about what had transpired the night before. It was too humiliating.

"I told you before that we're stuck here! You can just be thankful you're alive. I was lucky to reach you before you disappeared entirely. I couldn't believe anyone could be so stupid! Cold water kills quickly, little girl. I barely got to you in time." The harsh condemnation in his voice made her shiver. She agreed that she had been a victim of her own stupidity. How could she have skied so far? She had known that she had been gone from the lodge for hours, but the inclines had carried her swiftly over the snow and she hadn't known exactly when she had lost sight of the little red flags that marked the cross-country trail.

"Do you realize how badly you scared me?" he demanded. "You were delirious, and I'm no doctor. Considering that I held your shaking body in my arms the whole damn night, I think I'm entitled to know your name."

Appalled, she stammered, "Raine . . . Raine Morgan."

It sounded as if he were testing the two halves of her name as he muttered them out loud several times. "Never heard of you," he declared with what could only be called suspicion. Why did he think he should know her?

"Then we're even. I don't know you and you don't know me." She began edging her legs over the side of the bed, making sure the quilt kept them adequately covered as she tried to stand up. Her legs began to quiver as she placed her bare feet on the floor, and she had to sit back down on the bed. She was upset at her show of weakness and her eyes darkened angrily. She snatched at the loose covering and drew it around herself. Even with the heat rising from the cast-iron stove and the still-flickering glow from the huge stone fireplace, the room was frostily cold. It was an antiquated cottage and evidently had no outside modern heat source. The man who watched her every movement like some hawk circling its timid prey didn't seem affected by the brisk atmosphere inside the cabin. He had even pulled up the sleeves of his dark green, cable-stitched sweater, showing the golden brown hair on his arms.

"What's your game, Miss Morgan?" He interrupted her perusal of her austere surroundings. "Will I be confronted soon with a melee of reporters anxious to hear about my hermit life?" He stood up as he said it, bringing his foot to the chair seat and resting his arms on his knee. Something struck a chord in her head. His position on the chair, the casual gesture of his hands locked around one knee looked familiar. She tried to recall where she might have seen this man before, and as the dawning struck, her eyes widened with awe.

"You're Devlin Paige," she whispered, amazed that she was staring at one of the country's foremost entertainers. He looked exactly as he had on his last album cover, staring at her with his mesmerizing sherry eyes, his knee bent on a chair, an open-necked sweater revealing a strong brown throat. "You are really Devlin Paige?" She supposed she would have been better off to keep her recognition a secret, for the instant his name passed her lips, the chair went flying across the room and he looked ready to strangle her with his bare hands.

"You've made a bad mistake, Miss Morgan. You should have used that wide-eyed appeal the second you saw me. Then, I might have believed your unoriginal excuse for ending up here with me. I'm sure going swimming in January wasn't part of your plan, but ending up in my bed was the ultimate goal you had in mind, wasn't it? Too bad you weren't up to the lovemaking that usually goes with lying naked in my arms. When I find out what you're after, I might give you that pleasure."

"Your popularity has gone to your head, Mr. Paige! I have no intention of sleeping with you." What kind of man was he? She was determined to get dressed, offer her thanks and find a way to get back to the lodge as quickly as possible.

"Is that so?" Devlin responded to the uncertainty in her voice. "An odd comment to make when all you have on is a blanket." This time when his warm eyes slid across her naked shoulders, Raine forced back her responsive blush. Devlin Paige could have any woman he chose and certainly didn't need her to fill his bed. She smiled tremulously at him, hoping to appeal to his chivalrous nature, unaware of the effect of her smile. Clutching her covering, she walked over to her clothes and removed them from the line; holding them in a tight wad, she turned toward the bathroom. He seemed about to stop her; but when she walked bravely away from him, giving him her back, he hesitated and she was able to gain the relative security of the bathroom. She heard his deep chuckle as she hastily slid the latch into place on the door, her breath coming in rapid pants. He called, "The coffee is done. I'll give you five minutes and then I'll come in after you."

Raine needed no other incentive to dress swiftly. Shivering from the cold, she put on her underwear and rapidly buttoned her jersey shirt. Pulling her colorful ski sweater over her head, she dragged on her thick pants and slid her feet into the piled woolen socks. She wiggled her numbed toes in relief as the knitted covering brought instant warmth.

Above the washbasin hung a small mirror, and she peered at her face, hoping she didn't look a complete wreck. Although she was not one of his multitude of fans, she did admit that Devlin Paige was incredibly handsome. She recalled reading that he wrote his own music, and Raine had often thought that he should have let some other singer sing the lyrics. All Paige had going for him was a roguish, sensual face and a physique that set the women who clamored for seats at his shows into frenzied fits. Personally, Raine found such adulation disgusting, although she was forced to admit there was something so alluring about him that even she could feel the intrinsic pull on her senses. Still, he didn't have to worry that she was some worshipful admirer who would sell herself cheaply in order to tell her friends that she had slept with the great Devlin Paige.

She found a comb on the top of the pine table that held the porcelain basin, and used it to restore order to her golden curls. She dipped some water from a large bucket that stood under the table into the makeshift sink, and rinsed her face. Her skin was smooth, but yesterday's bout with the wind had given her a sun-kissed look that put color in her cheeks. A sprinkle of freckles crossed her upturned nose, and her wide, long-lashed brown eyes needed no artifice. She found a tube of toothpaste inside the medicine chest and used her finger for a toothbrush. After dumping the contents of the basin into another bucket in the corner of the small bathroom, she glanced again at her reflection in the mirror. She bit her lips until her soft mouth looked fragilely pink, and decided she was as ready as possible under the circumstances.

He was sitting at the round wooden table when Raine came out of the bathroom. His mocking eyes followed her progress across the room, lingering with amusement on her stocking feet with her loudly patterned red wool socks. She glanced down at her toes ruefully and issued the first genuine laugh since her vacation had begun. "Are my boots dry?"

"Dry, but shrunk to half their original size and as stiff as a board. If you plan to leave, you'll be doing it in those outrageous socks."

He knew she couldn't go anywhere without his help. It would be insane to try walking through the snow in a pair of wool socks. Her brows came together in a worried frown and her laugh broke off. Warily sitting down on the opposite chair he indicated, she picked up the brown earthenware mug of hot coffee that was waiting for her and saw that he had made breakfast while she was in the bathroom. A bowl of oatmeal and several pieces of charred-looking bread were placed before her. Though famished, Raine ignored the unappetizing consistency of the gruel and tried a bite of the blackened toast.

"You cook no better than you sing," she said without thinking, and then gave a little gasp as she realized how rude she had been. "I—I mean..." She floundered, meeting his astounded gaze with embarrassed shock. How could she have said such a terrible thing? His laugh was loud and deep chested, coming from somewhere inside him like a volcanic eruption. He seemed genuinely amused with her guileless statement, and Raine was completely bemused by the look on his face.

"At last, an honest woman," he declared, and picked up his coffee mug, giving her a theatrical salute with the steaming cup.

"You didn't mind?" she had to ask, astonished that he wasn't furious.

"Why should I mind? To some extent that's the truth. Perhaps you'll take over kitchen detail until I decide what's to be done with you." She chose to ignore the implied threat and pressed on.

"Being nothing but a sex symbol appeals to you?" she asked, no longer caring that her rudeness was becoming more pronounced. She felt justified, since he was deliberately taking advantage of the female populace to make money, his provocative music being only a means to that end.

He choked on his coffee. "I do happen to write my own music," he said after he regained control of himself. "I hold a degree in composition from Juilliard." Despite his earlier amusement, his temper had risen very close to the surface and was waiting to explode if she pressed him further. He was waiting for the inevitable compliment about his lovely music, but she had no intention of giving it to him.

"Nobody listens to your music when they can look at that body," she said simply, and saw that she had flummoxed him yet again. His jaw worked, and with difficulty he posed his next question.

"Are you saying that I remain on the charts because of the way I look?"

"Exactly," she answered, "just like Gloria Dexter does. She can't sing a note, but her records are bought because the young men who purchase them can gaze at her beautiful body on the cover and fantasize about her."

"Why you little—that's rubbish! Some women may buy my records for that reason, but it's my music that earned three gold records. I write damned good music!" He was really outraged, and Raine couldn't help feeling amused. She wondered if Devlin Paige had any real talent or if his ego was so large that he couldn't handle the truth about himself. Confined inside a small cabin with him, she needed to find some way to keep him at arm's length. "Do you have any of my albums?" he shot at her, pacing back and forth beside his chair.

"Not one. I only buy albums by singers who can sing. Why should I listen to someone who's shouting at me, when I can be soothed by the melodic tones of others?" She stared at him, her honest answer reflected in the wide brown eyes that refused to back down under his furious glare.

"So, you don't imagine yourself in my bed?" he continued relentlessly.

"Hardly. I'm looking for something more than a perfect body and a handsome face. As far as I can tell, that's all you have going for you." She hoped he would now throw her out of the cabin. Of course he would have to offer her something for her feet, but he certainly wouldn't be anxious to have her stay now that he knew how she felt about him. A man's ego was a fragile thing and she had just dented his severely. She didn't like the feeling that her immediate future was in the hands of this man, but she was certain that his conceit wouldn't tolerate making love to a woman who made no bones about the fact that she considered him less than talented, and no more than a pretty face. She couldn't let him see that she was just as affected by his handsome face and perfect body as the next woman.

"If that's how you feel, then why the hell did you accept this assignment? Or is all this just a means to get me to give you an exclusive—the honey didn't work, so the next step is a little vinegar?" His fascinating eyes probed her features, and she lifted her cup of coffee and took a calming sip before she answered him. She was going to need all of her strength to resist the hypnotizing appeal of the man. She wasn't half as immune to his compelling good looks as she wanted him to believe.

"I'm not on assignment, but I am a reporter and—" she began to tell him how she came to be here, but his ejaculation stopped her in midsentence.

"Aha! Just as I thought. Well, I'm not falling for this little strategy either. I have no need to defend my music, it defends itself."

"Vegetables!" Raine stated sharply, keeping her gaze steady as she watched his face.

"What?" At least he had heard her. "What did you say?"

"I write about food. Curried lamb, new ways of doing vegetables, things like that."

"And you want to interview me about what I like best to eat?" That seemed to amuse him and his temper calmed immediately. His mouth softened into a relieved smirk and Raine felt herself twitch with annoyance at his astounding conceit. "I thought you were after an in-depth interview. I guess I can spare you a few minutes to describe my favorite foods, since we're trapped inside this cabin until the plows can get through to us from the main road."

"Why on earth should somebody care what you like to eat?" She shook her head in disbelief. If he wasn't so full of his own importance, she would have felt genuine amusement when his eyes widened and his mouth dropped open.

"You just said that you were a food reporter," he exploded, coming around the table to stand by her side, looming over her with a self-contained violence that would have frightened her if she wasn't becoming angry herself. Somebody should have told him long ago that the world didn't revolve around him.

"Food editor," she corrected. "That doesn't mean I give a hoot what the famous Devlin Paige puts in his stomach. If it'll make you feel better, I'll write down what you eat and give it to our gossip columnist. Maybe she'll think your eating habits are newsworthy, but I have better things to do with my time." This conversation was totally ridiculous and suddenly Raine couldn't help laughing. She brought both hands to her mouth to stifle her giggles, but it didn't help. "It...it must be terrible..." she was laughing so hard that tears were streaming down her cheeks "having to worry if your dinner is worthy of your reputation. Do you keep up your image with a steady diet of oysters, Mr. Paige?" Raine let her mind loose on the possibilities. "I can see the headline: 'Sorry, ladies, but our Devlin eats lumpy oatmeal for breakfast. It sticks in his throat just like the words to his songs.'" She had forgotten that he stood right next to her as her imagination ran riotously with the idea of a female public clamoring for news about his likes and dislikes in food. "'Burnt toast is a favorite. He claims that charcoal is good for the suggestive gyrations he makes on stage.'"

Her laughter stopped abruptly and her stomach plummeted when she was dragged up out of her chair and hauled against his powerful body. He towered over her. She pushed against his chest but his hands held her shoulders tightly. "Enough!" he snarled between locked teeth. Their eyes met and held. Hers,

wide with alarm, were trapped beneath the
tigerlike gold flecks in his. A tremor coursed
through her as his expression softened and his
gaze moved from her eyes to her mouth.
"Lovely," he murmured, and her knees went
weak. His face moved closer and she swayed
toward him. His hands loosened their grip on
her shoulders. One hand twisted in the long
golden rope of her hair and the other spread
across her back to press her closer to his chest.
His mouth covered hers, claiming every soft
curve with firm possession. The galloping beat
of his heart pounded against her breasts and
she responded to the wild rhythm by helplessly opening her mouth and arching her body
closer to his. Her hands slid up his chest and
around his neck. He smelled all male, felt all
male and tasted delicious. Abruptly, he broke
off the embrace and stepped slightly away, his
breathing heavy and ragged.

She had been only seconds away from completely melting in the all-consuming fire of his
kiss. Never had her pulse raced so swiftly or
her mouth tingled with such disturbing heat.
She faced him, her eyes shocked and dazed,
watching as color ran up beneath his cheeks.
"I lost my temper." He let her go and strode to

the door of the cabin, dragging it open. A blast of frigid air and snow hit him squarely in the face. He wiped his face and cursed when he eyed the packed snow at the entrance, which showed him he would not be able to leave without some delay. "Looks like we're stuck, Miss Morgan. If you don't want a repeat of what just happened, try to keep your opinions about me to yourself."

Raine sat down on the chair to hide the quivering in her long legs. She stared into her coffee mug, unable to look at Devlin. She heard him poking around in the fireplace and stole a glance. He was placing new wood on the low-burning embers, ignoring her as she was ignoring him. Finally, he stood up and her heart began pounding as his lean body uncoiled its length from his position on the floor. They were trapped together inside the warm confines of this small cabin, and it looked as if there was nothing to do but make the best of it. She had to show him she was willing to forget what had just happened and behave civilly. "Do you have a supply of food?"

"Enough for about a week." He came to sit down opposite her. "Since you've made your distaste of my cooking known, perhaps you'd like to look around and fix something else for yourself."

"I don't usually eat breakfast. Are you still hungry?"

He brushed a stray lock of dark hair from his forehead, and she heard him suck in his breath with resignation. "Beggars can't be choosers. I'm quite sick of lumpy oatmeal and, believe it or not, I've never been conceited about my cooking abilities."

"Just your voice." Raine apologized immediately for the slip. "I'm sorry. That was unforgivable. I just didn't expect to be spending my vacation inside a remote cabin with *you*."

"This is a planned vacation?" he asked after a few minutes of uncomfortable silence.

"Yes." She straightened her spine as if to defend herself.

"You can understand why I jumped to the wrong conclusion, can't you?" He didn't like admitting that he finally believed her, but his mouth quirked as he watched the effort she had made to hide the pleased lift of her lips.

"I heard you sing once on TV. The cameras showed you being mobbed after the performance. I didn't think you'd get off the stage

alive,'' she said, drinking her coffee and casually refilling his cup with fresh brew.

"Why?"

"Why what?'' she asked, wondering what
he was trying to find out.

"If you don't enjoy my singing, why did you
watch one of my performances?''

"I like the lyrics to your songs. If you
don't . . . ah . . . lose your temper again, I'll tell
you something else.'' She didn't know why, but
she suddenly wanted him to know how much
she liked his music.

"I promise.'' His voice was dull. Though
still obviously annoyed by her candid opinions, he grudgingly allowed her to continue.

"I closed my eyes and listened to the lyrics
and the melody. I tried to imagine that it was
Randy Burke's voice that I was hearing. He
could really do justice to the wonderful words
in your songs by just slowing them down a bit
and singing them more like a ballad. When
you did 'Sunshine Past,' I imagined it was Neil
Diamond.''

"Thanks a hell of a lot,'' he said, definitely
offended. "You just can't stop, can you?''

"You did ask,'' she reminded softly, and
was surprised to see him smile.

"Remind me to tell you to lie next time."
His self-mocking expression made her laugh
and, unbelievably, he joined in.

"I've never met a woman like you before,
Raine Morgan," he remarked, almost to himself. "Most women would have complimented
me on my work, and then tried to seduce me if
they found themselves in my bed. All you've
done is told me what a fat head I've got."

"It looks good on you," she said honestly,
and could have bitten off her tongue.

His laughter erupted again and she was surprised to see he wasn't angry. "You are priceless! Whatever else we've got in store for us in
the next few days, it won't be boring." He gave
her a measuring look, then took an inventory
of her features, beginning with her eyes and
slowly drifting down to rest at the rise of her
breasts.

Uncomfortably aware of the trend of his
thoughts, she blurted, "You think it will be
that long before we get out?"

He leaned back in his chair, folded his arms
across his chest and gave her a mocking leer.
"Might be a week. We'll just have to make the
best of it."

Raine gulped, hiding her agitation. How could she be close to him for so long a time without begging him to make love to her? She had felt something in his arms she hadn't believed possible—a surge of feeling that left her craving his touch, yearning for the taste and smell of him—and he was making it clear that he wanted her.

Two

"What on earth are you doing in an isolated cabin in the north woods in Minnesota? I should think you would be far more comfortable in the Bahamas at some luxury hotel."

Devlin gave a disgusted snort that made her blink. "I hate all the hoopla that goes along with being an entertainer. This place is owned by a friend of mine, Patricia Blake. She offered me the cabin for a few days of relaxation. I wanted to be alone to write some songs, so I took her up on it."

"You know Patricia Blake?" Raine's disbelief was apparent in her tone. Patricia Blake was one of the world's finest operatic voices; yet Devlin spoke her name so casually.

The corners of Devlin's mouth lifted. "Considering your poor opinion of my musical ability, I'm not surprised you find it strange that Patricia and I are friends. I've been a fan of hers since I was a music student, and after opening night at the Met a few years ago, I went backstage to introduce myself and add my praise to her performance." He took a long sip of his coffee. There was a decided twinkle in his eyes when he continued, "As incredible as it may seem, I discovered that she was a fan of mine."

"You're kidding." The words were out before Raine could stop them. His response to her statement was a deep chuckle.

"It seems that Miss Blake, unlike some I might name—" he paused significantly, grinning "—believes I have talent. Unfortunately, she has more faith in my ability than I do. I haven't written one note since I settled in." He pointed to the guitar propped on the wall near the fireplace. "I'm finding it hard enough to survive on my own cooking and handle being away from the press without doing anything else.''

It was Raine's turn to chuckle. ''Considering your cooking ability, I can understand that you might have trouble composing while your stomach is growling at you. The least I can do to repay you for saving my life and giving me shelter during this storm is to cook a few decent meals. Are you writing the music for Patricia Blake's film? I remember reading something about her life story being done. Have you ever considered just composing?''

Raine was startled when Devlin abruptly stood up from his chair, the smile having vanished, replaced by a furious glare. ''What have you heard about my composing that score?'' His voice was little beyond a snarl, and Raine was at a total loss to explain his sudden change of mood.

''Nothing. I . . . I only asked because I think that's where your real talent lies.'' Her eyes widened as he rounded the table toward her. When he stopped inches from her, she recalled the results of the last time she had angered him. Her lips were still tingling from his kiss. She felt a shudder run down her spine and kept her gaze away from his face, focusing on the wall beyond the table. "I told you before that I think your lyrics and melodies are beautiful. It's just your voice singing them that I criticized."

The tension in his body eased slightly and he started back to the chair he had vacated, muttering, "That had better be all there is to it." Raine didn't understand what he meant, but didn't dare question his statement for fear of annoying him further.

Odd that he'd get so angry about a question about composing.... Why, I may have stumbled on a real scoop, she thought. Devlin Paige may be hiding away in the north woods to compose the score for the Patricia Blake story, but he doesn't want the public to know. She could feel her excitement grow at the prospect of writing a story that dealt with a real person and not the latest magic recipe. Just as quickly her enthusiasm fled—anything he had told her had been because he believed she was not after a story; so it would be unethical for her to report her discovery. Damn! she thought to herself. Here's my big chance, and I have to let it pass by. She eyed him warily, hoping he couldn't read her mind. She tensed when he looked at her, but relaxed when he sat down and refilled both their mugs, then smiled.

"I'm sorry if I frightened you. I'm getting paranoid about reporters, and you have admitted to being one."

"Not exactly a reporter," she prompted. "Racks of lamb don't offer much in an interview." Her remark was rewarded with a hearty laugh, and they spent the rest of the morning feeling each other out on a variety of subjects, carefully avoiding any references to his career. Raine was surprised to find how knowledgeable Devlin was in many areas. After a lengthy discussion about current political developments, he began to question her about her background. He seemed genuinely interested when she described her parents' farm, and plied her with questions about the dairy industry, as well as the small town where she grew up.

Raine, in turn, questioned him about his studies at Juilliard, trying not to sound like an interviewer. She found it increasingly difficult to concentrate on the content of his conversation. His voice was fascinating and she couldn't help thinking it was a shame he didn't sing the way he talked. There was a husky drawl in his deep baritone voice that played upon her nerves like fingers on a tightly drawn violin. Everything about him was a sensual treat.

His long, well-kept fingers on the coffee cup drew her attention, and she found herself remembering what they had felt like caressing her. She avoided looking directly at him because his eyes were too hard to withstand, the slumbering question hidden in their depths too compelling to deny very long. She knew that to survive for any length of time in this cabin, she couldn't succumb to a powerful pair of bedroom eyes. It was far safer to concentrate on a spot just beyond his head than to look directly at him. She told him about her vacation and how sick she was of her previous month's long involvement with asparagus tips. He shouted with laughter when she explained that this vacation was to relax her to the point where she could devote all her energy to Brussels sprouts when she returned to her desk at *Today's Woman.*

"You have less than I to brag about," he teased. "So far all I've seen is a great body, a beautiful face and a strange fascination for vegetables."

His sudden reference to her body had to be in retaliation for the personal remarks she had made about his earlier on. The remarks, coupled with the change in his voice, were totally unexpected; and her eyes flew to his face to find him giving her figure another thorough inspection. Color swept over her cheeks. "It's my job," she managed to say. "It's not very fair of you to refer to last night. I feel enough like an idiot as it is."

"You can dish it out, but you can't take it." He raised his brows. "As I remember, you enjoyed telling me that I've got a good body. I'm returning the compliment. Yours is good *all* over." His voice dropped suggestively lower as he made his last remark, and his eyes followed a path down her throat to the curve of her breast beneath her ski sweater.

"Let's keep this impersonal, Mr. Paige." Devlin Paige on the defensive was fascinating; turning on the charm, he was intriguing; but, on the offensive, he was devastating and beyond her experience.

"By all means—but I do find it silly to call you Miss Morgan, when I've run my hands over nearly every inch of you. Call me Devlin. Perhaps you'll mention me to the next man you sleep with. Darryl, Bob and now Devlin. If he feels as I did when I held you close for hours and heard you call me by another man's name, he'll probably throw you right out on the floor.''

Raine couldn't get her breath, sure she was going to die of embarrassment right on the spot. ''You...you don't have to insult me, Mr. Paige. If you'll excuse me, I'll fix us some lunch and you can take it as payment for what you did for me last night. I'd appreciate it if you wouldn't make it sound as if we...like you and I had made...'' Horrified, she couldn't finish the sentence, and he pounced on her childish lapse with real enjoyment.

''Made love?'' He filled in her blank. ''What if I told you that I fell in with your make-believe last night? Perhaps I didn't mind making love to a woman who had me confused with someone else. Especially when she's a woman built like you.'' The gold flecks in his eyes were dancing with pure mischief, but Raine was too upset to read them.

''What are you saying?'' Her question came out in an appalled squeak.

''I'm saying that I went along with your dreams, Raine. After seeing what you were like beneath your sodden clothes, I discovered that your fantasy closely resembled my own.''

"We did not make love!" she declared loudly, standing up like an outraged virago.

"How do you know? It might have been me that you were enjoying so much in your dreams—not Darryl, not Bob, but me.''

"That's where you're wrong!" she blurted. "If I had been with you, believe me I would have known!" She was emphatic, sure that her subconscious would not betray her to such an extent. With one kiss he had proved to her that she would never forget him. If he had made love to her, the feel of him would be branded on her for all time.

His satisfied smirk infuriated her further. "Good. That's all I wanted to know." His smile was wide and flashing. "I like to leave my women with an indelible impression. I'm glad that you're honest enough to admit that you wouldn't have forgotten me." He continued to grin as he sauntered to the bathroom.

She was left staring at the closed bathroom door, her eyes wide, her mouth open, looking exactly as he had looked when she had leveled him with her estimation of his singing ability. Thankfully, she had almost fifteen minutes to compose herself before he returned. She pretended to be concentrating on the sandwiches she was grilling atop the large black range.

"What's for lunch?" His voice came from somewhere close behind her, and inner radar told her that he was deliberately antagonizing her with his nearness, pleased that he had forced her awareness of him out into the open. "I'm told a cook should wear one of these," he continued as she stubbornly ignored him and he placed a ruffled loop over her head.

"What are you doing?" She gasped as his hands slid intimately around her waist and deftly crossed the apron strings in front, before bringing them behind her to tie them tightly in a bow. The apron was much too large and she guessed that he sometimes wore it himself. Her suspicion was confirmed when he said, "Looks much better on you than on me."

"Mr. Paige."

"Devlin," he insisted, keeping her trapped between the heated stove and his body. Fed up with the game he was playing, she twisted around in the small area left open to her, but discovered her mistake when she looked up and found him staring at her mouth.

"Will you leave me alone?" she snapped, pushing at the arms which came down on either side of the stove and kept her trapped against his chest.

"Not until you call me by my first name," he answered, knowing her only choice was to agree. She could smell the heady fragrance of a musky aftershave lotion and realized that he had just applied it on cheeks that no longer showed the auburn haze of a night's growth.

"Go to hell, Devlin," she said sweetly, and was gratified to see an infuriated glimmer darken his hazel eyes before he backed away.

"Mind if I eat first? I hate traveling on an empty stomach." The flame in his eyes died as he surveyed the sandwiches she had placed on a large platter. Quite willing to ignore the suggestive incident, Raine gestured to the table. He quickly took his place and she served him the large sandwich, grilled to perfection. Melted cheddar cheese oozed out of the golden crust and he looked as if he might devour the thing in one mouthful. He finished his sandwich in less time than it took her to swallow three bites.

"Haven't you eaten anything decent for a while?" she asked, as he greedily eyed the remaining half of her sandwich.

"You already know I'm a rotten cook. I didn't think there was much to it, and was I ever proved wrong. In the week that I've been here, I've managed that oatmeal, canned soup and peanut-butter sandwiches. I'm starving." Not once did his eyes leave the thick sandwich on her plate, and she gave a resigned sigh.

"Here, stop salivating." She couldn't help but laugh at the grateful expression on his face when she handed him her plate.

"Would you like a job?" he managed to ask between bites.

"I have a job," she answered automatically. Of all things he could have said, asking her to work for him was the last thing she expected. Her curiosity got the better of her after a short silence. "Why would you offer me a job?"

"Several reasons. First, I'm starving and you seem to be an expert on food and its preparation. Next, I assume you can type since you are a reporter—" he flashed her a quick smile "—rather, an editor. I told you I was trying to compose—without much luck—and I need your help," he pleaded mournfully.

"I'll prepare our meals while we're stuck here, but beyond that I think I'm better suited to my work at the magazine." She resisted the basset-hound appeal in his eyes.

"Please hear me out," he pleaded with seeming sincerity, his gaze intent on her face. "You have one very important asset—you're not enamored of me. The last woman I hired lasted three hours. That's when I went to relax in my Jacuzzi and discovered my tub was already occupied, and accompanied by an open invitation."

"You're kidding!" Raine ignored both his job offer and his opinion that she was not "enamored" and focused her thoughts on the woman in his hot tub. "Does that sort of thing happen often?"

"Too often to count," he muttered, avoiding her gaze.

She could almost feel sorry for him, but working with him was out of the question. He was mistaken if he thought she was not attracted to him—how long would it be before she, too, was issuing an open invitation?

"I'll stick with Brussels sprouts, thank you." However, her refusal seemed only to increase his desire to have her working for him. He named a ridiculously generous figure for a starting salary and offered her a chance at writing an in-depth article about him for *Today's Woman*.

"The experience you could get by working for me would be of enormous help to your career." He continued dramatically, "Look, I'm desperate. I type with two fingers, I'm wasting away to nothing and I don't want some dizzy broad who will flatter my ego every two minutes."

"Dizzy broad?" Raine's hackles rose dangerously. "If that's how you refer to any member of my sex, the answer is a positive, capital NO."

He didn't sound entirely sincere in his apology and she told him to drop the subject—but was the tiniest bit disappointed when he shrugged his shoulders and stood up from the table to begin clearing the dishes. What had she wanted him to do? Get down on his knees and beg? She was certain that any experience she would gain from working for him would not be the kind that would build her career. If she ever did work for him, she would have to constantly fight the undeniable attraction he held for her. Her senses went into a tailspin every time he opened his mouth and smiled at her with the darkened, dreamy eyes of a lover. Stop it, you dizzy broad, she chastised herself and laughed with self-derision. She picked up her plate and walked to the sink. He was using the pump at the side to fill a large kettle with water. He carried it to the stove and settled it there to heat for washing the dishes.

She busied herself by scraping the plates, which held nothing but bread crumbs. She could feel his eyes assessing her as she began wiping the counter tops with a damp cloth.

"If I'd done more than give you the universal treatment for hypothermia, you wouldn't have turned down my offer."

Her eyes shot up to find his again tracing a line down her throat to the neckline of her bulky sweater, then continuing until he had scanned her entire figure. Grateful for the thick material that covered her and effectively hid her body's reaction, Raine frowned furiously. "Will you kindly stop using your sex-symbol image to get to me. First you offer me a job because you want someone who isn't interested in you as a man, then you suggest that if we had made love I'd have accepted the job. Just who is the dizzy one around here?''

His deliberately provocative perusal and the inviting stance of his lean body had probably brought other women to him on the run. His voice had never sounded more suggestive, low and drawling while his eyes flickered her full breasts to life with flaming probes from gold-flecked irises. She almost felt like loosening the collar of her shirt and wiping her brow to remove the almost perceptible heat of his gaze. No wonder he made millions at his concerts. This pull on her responses was irresistible. Her temper rose when she realized he was doing it deliberately.

"Most effective," she finally managed through gritted teeth as his eyes caressed her. "But I'm not buying it or the job offer. I outgrew my fascination for stars years ago. Besides, redheads aren't my type." Her tone was dismissing, and this time she got an immediate reaction. He picked up the kettle of water and angrily poured the steaming contents into the sink. He threw her a dish towel and began washing their dishes irately. He wasn't speaking to her—not with his eyes, his voice or anything else. Raine found it a peculiarly childish reaction from a man who was in no way a child. When they had silently completed the dishes and put them away, Raine decided to move as far back from his stonily angry presence as possible. By the look of it, he had never been turned down by a woman before. It must be wonderful to generate the kind of sexual power he did, she thought jealously. Imagine what it would be like to lower her voice, stand slightly different, then stare beguilingly and have men falling all over themselves to get to her.

She escaped the kitchen area, and sat down in an old-fashioned cane-seated rocker before the fireplace and gazed into the flickering flames. She made no attempt to engage him in further conversation; his mere presence made her heart flutter painfully. She sensed him standing behind her and the hair on her nape stood up, but he didn't touch her. He walked to the only other chair, a comfortable-looking overstuffed armchair covered with a rust-colored rough fabric, and sat down. The silence became unbearable. She could almost feel his will working inside her. He wanted her to say something that would soothe his frayed ego. Stubbornly, she refused and remained silent. She forced herself to think about what she would do once she got safely back to the hotel. She didn't want to continue a vacation that had turned out to be the most unsettling experience she had ever endured—discounting her harrowing brush with death. She would never be able to listen to another Devlin Paige song without recalling his lips on hers and that she had once lain naked in his arms.

"It's going to be a very long day if this keeps up," Devlin finally interjected into the silence that had been broken only by the crackle of the fire and the occasional creak of the rocker. His temper seemed to have disappeared and his voice sounded amused. She swung her face around, pushing the gold strands of hair off her cheek as she smiled weakly. "I'm willing to be pleasant if you are."

He sat forward in the chair and bent over to rest his elbows on his knees. He clasped his hands together between his legs as he stared at the hardwood floor. "Do you know something, Raine? I like you. You're the first woman to turn me down in a long time. I'm sorry for my earlier behavior. It's just that I've gotten so used to having any woman I was interested in say yes, that I'd honestly forgotten how it felt to be turned down." He raised his gaze to hers. She was startled by the look of unhappiness she saw there. "I've lived too long in the fast lane, I guess."

Raine was unsure where he was heading with this conversation. A part of her wanted to reach out and comfort him and ease the... what? What did his look imply? Loneliness? He, who was constantly surrounded by a large retinue and adoring fans?

"I was serious about the job offer. You might sorely try my temper, but so far you haven't gotten on my nerves." His hazel eyes showed his frustration and she felt an immediate sympathy, but she couldn't help him. Even as his employee, she wouldn't fit into the life he led. They were worlds apart—almost galaxies. She had to point out their irreconcilable differences and be honest about the strongest reason why she couldn't work for him.

"I am a card-carrying member of the press," she emphasized. "It wouldn't work and you know it. I enjoy my job on the magazine and, besides, before very long we would probably be lovers. I couldn't handle something like that. You would move on to other women and I would be left with a sentimental memory of sleeping with a famous star. It's not enough for me.''

Her honesty both pleased and dismayed him. ''I knew that you felt it. You do, don't you?''

She looked away from the sherry-colored eyes that had held hers intoxicated by the warmth and longing she saw there. ''Yes.'' Her voice came in a whisper, and the soft, feminine sound of it brought a gratified light to his eyes. He studied the golden highlights in her hair and her profile for long moments, hoping that the storm outside would continue as the deep snow offered him the only real excuse he had for keeping her here as long as possible. He wanted her—for how long he couldn't be sure, but he wanted enough time with her to find out.

''Want to go outside and build a snowman?'' he asked, and the total change of subject made her shake her head with confusion.

''A snowman?'' she repeated, stupefied.

''Sure, haven't you ever made one?'' he frowned.

"Of course. I was raised in the Snow Belt, remember? I have plenty of experience in snow angels too. Winters are long in Minnesota. If you're from New York City, I should think you'd be the one to have difficulty making a snowman."

He stood up and reached for her hand, rushing her to the wooden doweled coatrack and into her ski jacket. Before she could utter a word, he jammed her tousle cap over her ears and grabbed her fur-lined gloves. She pulled them onto her trembling fingers and waited for him to button his coat. "I don't think you're quite ready to go out in the snow, Snow Princess." He looked down at her stocking feet and pulled a pair of boots from a closet. They were far too big; so he gave her a pair of his socks to stuff in each toe.

They had to dig themselves out of the cabin, and it took both of them working hard side by side to break through the huge drift of snow that blocked the door. By the time they were able to stand atop the ice-crested snow outside, they were panting from the exertion. Devlin took off his thick, down-filled jacket, leaving himself in his beautifully knit sweater. Flakes of crystallized powder glistened in his auburn hair and his tanned face glowed in the pale light of winter. The storm had abated somewhat, though it was still lightly snowing, with soft patterns of flakes falling from the heavy gray cloud cover.

"I hope the rest of this frolic is easier." He grinned, looking like a boy who had just discovered new territory to explore. Hadn't he played in snow before? Didn't he know what it was like to crunch through the deep quiet of a crystallized forest and wonder about the frosty magician who had created the fairyland?

She watched him smile up at the snow-filled gray clouds and take a deep breath of the pine-scented air. It was as if the very presence of nature made him happy. She had to admit that it was beautiful here, and she looked around her with new eyes. The trees formed a powder-puff awning of white over their heads. Wind moved the green fans of fir until huge floes of snow spilled from the branches and fell soundlessly upon the silvery light mattress covering the ground.

"It's wonderful, isn't it?" she asked, and took courage from his flashing grin. She bent to roll a small snowball in her glove. When she had made a nice round ball, she drew back her arm and threw. It hit him squarely in the chest and he looked back at the clinging white patch for a moment, perplexed. The next instant, she was running for cover behind a nearby tree as a retaliatory snowball smacked her shoulder. After that, it was a riotous free-for-all. His aim was letter-perfect, and before long Raine was covered with snow from her hat to the tops of her boots. She had the distinct impression that snowball fighting was not new to him. He might have admitted to being a city boy, but it did snow in the Big Apple, didn't it?

"Cease fire!" she shouted when his last missile landed behind her neck and the snow melted down inside the collar of her jacket. She peeped out from behind the cluster of birches where she had sought shelter from his deadly aim. He had disappeared. She stepped out from her meager defense and looked in both directions. Where had he gone so swiftly?

"Devlin? Sneak attacks are against the rules." At least they were in Minnesota. Her warning got no response from the deep silence of the snow-mulled forest. Her startled gasp as she was lifted off her feet from behind shot like a cannon through the noiseless wonderland of frost. She squealed as her body sailed through the air and was swallowed within a huge drift of clinging snow. She struggled up out of the frigid coldness, giggling at her abominable-snowman appearance. Covered from head to toe, she was weighted down by a thick coating of white crystals. Only her laughing face had escaped being coated.

"Not a bad snowman for my first attempt," Devlin laughed down at her, standing to survey his handiwork with his hands on his hips. She didn't wait for him to add more insult to injury, but sized up the drift behind him and charged like an avalanche, catching him in the chest. He was knocked off his feet, and disappeared under an equally deep drift.

At first she thought she had knocked the breath out of him because he lay without moving. His eyes were open and he was staring up at the winter sky. Then, she knew he wasn't hurt, for his lips held a serene smile. Caught up in the mood, she lay down beside him, listening to the soft sounds of the forest, delighted by the feel of melting snowflakes sifting across her face. She closed her eyes.

"Raine." The soft, husky pronouncement made her lift her lashes. He was propped up on

one elbow and was leaning over her, staring
into her face. Her lips parted, but before she
could speak her mouth was covered by his.
Wrapped in a snow-covered blanket, she was
warmed by his touch. They were lying in a fir-
fanned bed of soft white powder, an outdoor
boudoir as intimate as any bedroom. Icicle
flames burst and melted inside her as his
tongue licked the flakes of snow from her lips
and his dark eyes turned the intoxicating color
of brandy. He kissed her again and again, his
mouth running over her face, tasting the
snowflakes on her lashes and numbed cheeks.
She no longer felt shivers of cold race down
her spine, but hot waves of pleasure welling up
from deep inside. Helplessly, her hands ran up
his arms and across his broad shoulders, then
locked behind his neck, drawing him closer.
Her breath came out in a soft sigh of longing
as she lifted her head from the snow pillow and
used the tip of her tongue to flick the melting
crystals of snow from the edges of his lips.
When her tongue slipped into his mouth, he
immediately pressed her back upon the snow.
With a deep groan of male satisfaction, his
body covered hers. His powerful thighs straddled her legs, making her aware of the urgent

hardness of his desire. Their tongues met, his encircling hers enticingly until she was frantic for more. She was unprepared when he suddenly pulled away from her and sat up.

"We had better get inside before we both die of pneumonia," he stated matter-of-factly, and Raine felt worse than if he had slapped her. How could he sound so unmoved when she had still not quite returned from her fairy-tale wonderland? She scrambled unsteadily to her knees, and then to her feet.

"You're right. It is cold out here," she said, hoping the strangled murmur would not be recognized for what it was. Confused by her own reaction to his sudden withdrawal, she moved like an automaton to the door of the cabin, struggling through the deep snow in her large boots. She could hear his tread lagging, and glanced back to see him look reluctantly at the impressions they had left in the snow. She couldn't open the heavy door, and had to wait until he caught up with her and pushed it in. When she was able to get past him, she slipped inside the cabin and turned her back on him while she got out of her snow-covered outer clothes. The tears glimmering in her eyes were not caused by the cold alone.

It was no later than four in the afternoon, but it was rapidly growing darker. Neither of them spoke as they hung their coats on the line stretched near the fireplace. Raine sat down in the rocker to pull off her boots, half-filled with caked snow, and to strip off her wet socks. Devlin did the same in the opposite chair. She pulled off her sweater, and her eye caught on his long arms stretched over his head as he removed his. Their every action grew more intimate with each passing second.

The rest of her clothes were as sodden as her outer things. She knew they would soon be dripping as the heat of her body and the warmth from the fireplace melted the snow. The sensible thing would be to remove them all, but she would be forced to wrap herself in a blanket again and would feel that much more vulnerable. She had shown him outside that she wanted him, and she wanted him still. She began to shake as the cold clamminess of her clothes broke through the warm, passion-inspired haze that had gripped her. Then, he was beside her, pulling her up by her frozen hands.

"I want you, Snow Maiden," he murmured, as his fingers began unbuttoning her knit shirt. She was captivated by his liquid sherry eyes and could only nod mutely. She knew now that his swift turn away from her outside had meant he wanted much more than a kiss in the snow. His warm fingers slid the shirt from her shoulders and flung it onto the bed. His hands roamed freely over the smooth skin of her back as he drew her to him. His lips captured her mouth and he placed his hands over hers, guiding them to his waist and under the thermal knit of his shirt. She needed no further urging when her fingers felt the flat muscular skin of his stomach. He unfastened her ski pants and his hands moved below her waist and cupped her buttocks, pressing her to the reality of his hardened desire. His lips moved from her mouth to trace a searing trail across her cheek and down her throat. She clung to him, unable to respond to the warning bells shrieking in her head. Her body arched against him, all caution thrown aside.

His hands came up and his fingers fumbled with the clasp of her bra, as his lips returned to cover hers. A shudder shook her when he slipped the lacy bra away and cupped her naked breasts in his palms.

She heard a distant whining sound, but could concentrate on nothing but the enticing play of Devlin's fingertips upon her erect nipples. She moaned, softly, when his fingers tugged at her breasts and his large palms closed over her softness. The whining became insistent and was followed by a scraping noise outside the door. She lifted her head away from his and looked over his shoulder. Paying no attention to her distraction, Devlin took her movement away from his mouth as an invitation to kiss her throat.

The scratching became louder, but Devlin was oblivious. When his mouth enclosed one taut nipple, she gasped. Someone or something was outside and she had to get Devlin's attention. She tried to push the dark amber head away from her breast, but he was reluctant to release her and tightened his arm at her back.

"Devlin. There is something outside," she whispered fearfully.

"Wolfe," he muttered, as if that wild animal held no fear for him.

"A wolf?" she shrieked, and jerked out of his arms.

"All right, I'll let him in," he gritted from between clenched teeth. She reached out to stop him.

"No! Are you crazy?"

"I won't get any peace unless I let him in. He'll keep on whining until I open the door."

He strode to the door and pulled it open. A white snow-covered mound of fur bounded into the room, pausing only long enough to shake the worst of the snow from its coat, and then charged toward Raine. She screamed and staggered backward, losing her balance and toppling onto the bed, trying to ward off the gigantic German shepherd's enthusiastic greeting. He barked and leaped up beside her, throwing a heavy paw across her lap and leaning his massive head against her chest. A large red tongue began licking her neck.

Squealing and pushing the beast away, she looked to Devlin for assistance and found him struggling to contain laughter, with no success. "Down, Wolfe!" he commanded when he got his breath. The dog reluctantly obeyed, hopped off the bed and grudgingly trotted to the fireplace, where he circled several times before dropping down upon the hearth rug. He gave a sigh as he nestled his head on his paws and looked back at Raine with huge adoring brown eyes.

"That beast used to be my friend," Devlin muttered. Raine giggled at his satiric statement while slipping her arms back into her still-damp shirt. The spell was broken and she felt self-conscious in her state of half-nudity. Devlin showed every sign of ridding them of the canine pest and taking up where they had left off, but for Raine the mammoth shepherd's entrance had restored her scattered senses, giving her time to think. Devlin was not offering her anything beyond the promised pleasure of the moment, and she was painfully aware that she wanted far more than he was offering.

"Let him stay," she said as she crossed the room and knelt down beside the dog, trying not to notice Devlin's scowl when he shrugged his shoulders and turned away. He began rummaging in a drawer of the large oak dresser next to the bed and pulled out a shirt.

"Here, this is drier than the one you have on. The hairy fellow beside you is Wolfe. He brought me to your rescue yesterday and it looks as if he thinks he has prior claim." At the mention of his name, Wolfe wagged his tail enthusiastically and lifted his head, his tongue lolling out of his mouth in an expression of sheer joy.

Three

———

The next morning Raine crept out from under the warmth of the covers, let Wolfe out of the cabin, then ran to the bathroom. Her bare feet made little noise on the pine floor, for her movements were quick. The cabin was freezing and the floor felt as cold as a skating rink. She got a brief glimpse of Devlin sprawled beneath a mound of blankets on the short couch, his stocking feet hanging over the end. Her lips straightened to a line as she recalled the previous evening.

The furry newcomer to the cabin not only had interrupted a perfect seduction scene, but had provided a distraction for the entire evening. He had followed her around the cabin like a lapdog and Raine was able to concentrate her attention on Wolfe, outwardly ignoring any subtle attempts Devlin made to rekindle the fire Wolfe's entrance had extinguished.

Devlin had impatiently accepted Wolfe's presence and had explained that the dog came and went as he pleased. Raine owed Wolfe a lot. Not only had he brought Devlin to her rescue the day before yesterday, but had since saved her from something that might have been almost more devastating than the frigid river water. Without Wolfe's entrance and distracting presence, Raine knew she would have spent the night making love with Devlin. That she would have enjoyed it she was certain—but what about today and tomorrow?

Raine splashed cold water over her face and erased all signs of sleep from her eyes. She stared at the mirror, not seeing the reflection of her troubled face. What did she want from Devlin? She had just met the man—to think that she was in love with him was absurd.

But . . . whatever she felt would be ruined by a one-night stand.

She had wanted him desperately and understood that frustrated desire was behind Devlin's increasing bad temper the evening before. Hadn't she felt the same? Hadn't she fought a battle within herself all evening and most of the night? How easy it would have been to shoo Wolfe on his way, cross the cabin and be enfolded in Devlin's arms—to give herself up to his intoxicating kisses and pleasuring caresses. She shivered with the cold and the memory of the frozen glare Devlin had given her when she suggested that she take the couch for the night. He had angrily refused her offer and sarcastically suggested she share the bed with her new admirer. Muttering expletives under his breath, he had pulled blankets from a cupboard, thrown himself on the couch and pulled the blankets up over his head. She had fallen asleep after hours of tossing and turning, wondering if she had won or lost.

She replaced the face towel on the rack and decided to get dressed before she froze to death. Her feet were already numb. The flannel shirt Devlin had given her to wear reached only to her midthigh and offered scant com-

fort against the chilly air. Cautiously she
opened the bathroom door and peered at the
couch. Devlin was still sleeping; so she began
to tiptoe quietly past him to retrieve her
clothes, which were still on the line where she
had hung them the night before. She could
hear the howling wind screaming around the
corners of the cabin and wondered how much
longer she would be forced to remain. She was
certain that by now her parents would have
been notified of her disappearance and would
be sick with worry. She felt helpless, unable to
communicate with the outside world. A tight
knot of anxiety gripped her.

A resounding staccato knock burst into her
thoughts and Raine shrieked. Her startled
alarm brought Devlin off the couch in one
swift motion. They stood staring at each other
as the pounding came again. Not wanting to be
caught in nothing but a man's oversize shirt,
Raine ran back to the safety of the bathroom.
She kept the door open a crack as Devlin
pulled on a pair of pants. He yelled, ''I'm
coming,'' in a thoroughly disgruntled voice;
then, with his shirt still unbuttoned, he crossed
the cabin and pulled open the door. Raine was
mortified when her eyes darted to her lacy un-

derthings still hanging from the clothesline stretched in front of the fireplace. She hoped Devlin wouldn't let anyone come inside until he took down her clothes. She groaned with dismay when two tall men, dressed in uniforms of the Forest Service, stomped inside. She was a silent witness to their knowing expressions, as they surveyed the feminine underwear hanging before the fire and one of them nodded toward them as he stated his reason for being there.

"I hope those clothes belong to a certain Miss Morgan who was reported missing from the Piney Edge Lodge. The rangers have been scouring these woods for the past thirty-six hours. I'm Sergeant Hanks, and I'm leading the search." He held out his hand, and Devlin stared at it for several seconds before he assimilated the man's words. She could see the indecision on his face as he shook the man's hand. She didn't want him to admit that she was with him and had been for the last two nights, but the ranger's next words made that hope an impossibility. "Her folks are frantic. We saw this cabin and your smoke. Is she here?"

Before Devlin could answer him, the door was again pushed open and two men, one of them carrying a camera, burst into the cabin. "It's true!" A short, wiry man wearing a bright yellow stocking cap perched on top of his head spoke gleefully. "You're really Devlin Paige! We thought it was you when we looked in the window, but we couldn't believe our eyes. I'm Floyd Mattlock with the *Chronicle*. Can you imagine? Meeting Devlin Paige out here in these woods!" He took Devlin's hand and began pumping it up and down enthusiastically. "What a story! Did you arrange to meet Miss Morgan here? Is this your romantic hideaway from the world?"

Devlin's groan was lost in the barrage of questions that followed. Bulbs flashed and the camera whirred as the local reporter introduced his photographer. Evidently, news of Raine's disappearance had drawn the interest of the local newspaper and it had sent a reporter to follow up on the story. Expecting to find the unlucky victim of a winter blizzard, he had stumbled on an even bigger story. The famous Devlin Paige was staying unnoticed in the north woods and he wanted to know everything about it. Why had Devlin come? How long had he been in the region? When did he plan to leave? Interest in Raine became secondary, until the photographer tripped over the clothesline and got back to his feet with Raine's bra hooked to his sweater.

What followed was a humiliating scene that Raine would never be able to forget. Devlin grabbed her things and stuffed them under the covers of the bed. The reporter caught sight of the slightly open bathroom door and discovered her presence. Uncaring that he had crossed all bounds of common courtesy, unhampered by Devlin's furious protests and the forest ranger's warning for order, she was dragged from her sanctuary and bombarded with questions. Her face was etched in alabaster as Devlin angrily placed a coat over her shivering shoulders and then took a swing at Floyd Mattlock. The punch landed squarely on the startled reporter's jaw. Instantly a hush descended and the rangers hastily ushered the two newsmen out of the cabin. Sergeant Hanks told Devlin that he would get rid of the newspapermen, but then he would have to return to get some answers to a few questions about Raine's disappearance from Piney Edge

Lodge. The man gave her a curt nod as he swiftly shut the door behind him.

"Oh, God," Raine moaned, and sank down on the bed, hiding her tear-streaked face in her hands. Never had she felt so totally humiliated.

"Get dressed!" Devlin growled at her in a voice so savage she wanted to run. Mutely, she gathered her clothing together and took it inside the bathroom. She dressed rapidly, uncaring that her clothes were wrinkled and creased. She heard Sergeant Hanks come back inside, and grimaced when Devlin shouted though the door, "Come and explain to this officer how you got here."

Devlin seemed to have withdrawn from her and his eyes were like twin glaciers, matched only by the frozen expression on his face.

She explained her accident to the ranger, trying to impress him with the fact that she had no control over what had happened. She stated emphatically that if she had been able to return to the lodge or contact them, she would have done so immediately. Sergeant Hanks informed her that her parents were waiting for news at Piney Edge, and offered to take her back with him. The snowplows had opened the main road and were now gaining access to Devlin's cabin. The rangers and reporters had proceeded ahead of the plow on snowmobiles, suspecting that Raine might be taking refuge from the storm in the cabin. While they talked, she could hear the plow cutting its way toward them. As the sound of approaching civilization grew nearer, Devlin moved farther away. By the time Hanks offered to leave her alone with Devlin for a few minutes and stepped outside so she could make her goodbyes, Devlin had erected a barrier between them that she could not hope to scale. She put on her jacket and asked if she could wear his extra pair of boots. He gave her a brief affirmative nod, but she knew that his attention was elsewhere. She ended up offering him a miserable little speech of thanks for his hospitality, then almost ran to the door. His voice stopped her before she could step outside.

"This isn't the end, Raine," he stated, but there was nothing friendly in the prediction.

"It isn't?" She stared back at him, blinking back the tears that moistened her long lashes.

"They'll try to make the most of this situation. I hope you're up to the unmerciful hounding you may be in for." It sounded more like an accusation than a warning. She hadn't planned what had happened today. How could she have known?

"You won't be able to stay here now, will you?" she asked sadly.

He snorted sarcastically. "I've been here quite long enough, don't you think?"

"I'm so sorry." She didn't know what else she could say.

"Not half as sorry as I am." He turned his back on her and pulled a large rucksack from underneath the bed. Tears forced themselves between her lashes and rolled unheeded down her cheeks. He didn't have to speak so coldly to her. She had gotten his message loud and clear the minute he had ordered her into the bathroom to get dressed. He had no desire to have his name linked with some foolish little nobody from Minneapolis. She had provided him with a pleasant diversion for a short while, but she had ruined his idyllic retreat. Although none of what had happened had been strictly her fault, he had placed all blame squarely on her shoulders.

She opened the door and ran to the jeep that would take her back to the lodge. Sergeant Hanks suggested that if she wanted to avoid the crowd of other reporters who had based themselves at the lodge, waiting word of her being found, she could ride with him to the ranger station and he would relay a message to her parents to meet up with them there. Gratefully she accepted his kind offer, and an hour later she was enfolded in her mother's arms.

"Darling ... we were so worried." Caroline Morgan wiped a few thankful tears away from her brown eyes and offered her handkerchief to Raine so she could do the same.

"Are you all right?" Raine's father, John Morgan, asked in a gruff tone that told her he had feared the worst. She saw the lines of strain etched about his generous mouth and across his broad, weather-beaten forehead. She smiled tremulously up at him and went from her mother's arms into his. She gained little comfort from his hearty bear hug. When she was a child her tall, big-chested father had been able to protect her from all hurts, to soothe all injuries; but he could not soothe the pain now embedded in her heart. She shed a few more tears upon his strong shoulder and then asked to be taken home.

Five hours later they drove up to the white frame farmhouse where she had been born.

She still had four full days of vacation, plus the
weekend, before she had to return to the world
of food articles and recipes. She intended to
spend them in the secure setting of the farm,
where she hoped to forget her interlude with
Devlin Paige. All the way home in the car her
thoughts drifted, replaying every minute of the
past two days. She was grateful that her parents had asked few questions. She told them
most of what had transpired, only leaving out
anything that hinted at her famous cabin
mate's heady charm. She needed time—time to
forget her fierce reactions to Devlin's lovemaking and time to prepare for the questions
she would inevitably have to answer when she
returned to work. She would offer most people the truth and let them reach their own con-
clusions. Her friends would believe her and the
opinions of others didn't really matter very
much. She was hopeful the frantic phone call
she had made earlier to Sheila Hemmings, her
editor in chief, would discourage any nosy reporters from discovering her parents' address.
Their dairy farm was almost fifty miles west of
Minneapolis, and she doubted her involvement with Devlin would remain a newsworthy
item long enough for the reporters to want to

pursue the story that far in the attempt to track
her down. She had begged Sheila not to dis-
close her location to anyone. After two days
had passed without incident, Raine felt rela-
tively safe. She had promised Sheila a complete account of her astounding episode if she
got her word that it would be strictly off the
record.

She spent four quiet days trying to erase a
picture of sherry-colored eyes and stop remembering the feel of long tapered fingers
touching her pliant body. By the weekend she
had pretty much regained outward control of
her emotions. She didn't know how much
longer she could keep lying to herself and not
admit that she had fallen in love with a man
who she would probably never see again, or
who, if she did see him, would find he didn't
remember her.

On Saturday she drove into the small town
near her parents' farm. She ran into Bob Williams and his wife, Linda, and was pleased to
see that they seemed a happy couple, very
much in love. There was no embarrassment in
seeing Bob again and they enjoyed a nice chat
on Main Street before she told them she had to
complete a few errands for her mother. Some-

times she missed the simple setting of her childhood, missed the clean fragrant smell of hay in the fields and the friendly faces of the townspeople who had known her all her life. She walked into the Jacobs' Pharmacy to pick up her mother's blood-pressure medicine and smiled at Harold Jacobs, the proprietor, as she approached the counter.

"Raine Morgan! Good to see you. Home on vacation from that fancy magazine you work for? The ladies look for your articles every time we have a new edition come in. Miz Jacobs tries all your recipes. Those cookies in the Christmas issue sure were good."

"Thanks, Mr. Jacobs. I'll tell the test kitchen. I'm afraid I just write about them, the staff in the kitchen does the real work," Raine laughed. "This is my last day home. I've come for my mother's prescription." Her eyes warmed affectionately as the spritely old man picked up a nearby package and handed it to her, already filled.

"Thought Caroline would be by today," he admitted, and wrote in the large ledger beside the cash register. "On your dad's bill, Raine?"

She nodded and accepted the cherry sucker he held out in his other hand; it was her favor-

ite flavor. She had never left this store without
some sweet token from the pharmacist. How
he kept track of his customers' preferences was
a mystery to her; she hadn't been inside his
store in months. Her eyes roamed over the familiar soda fountain and the magazine racks.

"Think I'll look around," she said, as Mr.
Jacobs nodded and bent his head back to the
ledger. She strolled casually over to the magazine rack and began scanning the newspapers.
She picked up a paper from Minneapolis and
turned to the entertainment section. The paper was two days old. She anxiously looked
over the headlines but saw no mention of
Devlin anywhere. Extremely relieved, she
glanced at a national tabloid whose large-type
headlines caught her eye. Her breath stopped.
Devlin's face stared back at her from the front
page. He was smiling as only he could, his
magnetism and charm captured by the photographer. She picked up the paper and read
the caption for the enclosed article, which was
written in bold print across the top of the page.

"Mystery Woman Haunts Devlin's
Dreams." Inside, she quickly found the three-
page spread that explained the headline. Her
fingers shook as she read and digested the ap-

palling lies Devlin had spun about their time together. Several pictures showed Devlin as he had appeared that horrible morning in the cabin—Devlin with his shirttails fluttering to reveal his bare chest. Devlin stepping in front of the photographers to protect the bare-legged blonde whose face had escaped being photographed. She recognized the parts of her that were visible and her cheeks burned. She was not mentioned by name—which was hard to believe—but was referred to as a bewitching golden blonde who had appeared out of nowhere and disappeared as soon as the cabin had been invaded by the press. Devlin was reported to be devastated by the loss of the "ethereal beauty" who had slipped in and out of his life. "When we were discovered, she ran away," he was quoted as saying sadly.

There was not a word of truth in the whole article. He had managed to twist the story into an almost dreamlike mystery. Why had the reporters, who had obviously sold the story to the tabloid for a lofty sum, left out the details of her disappearance, her easily discovered name and occupation? It sounded as if she had been some kind of spiritual creature who may have existed only in Devlin's imagination. She read the ridiculous quotes he had given to the interviewer. "She came out of the night and lit up my life for only a moment before stealing away. I am at a total loss to explain. I have fallen in love with a beautiful spirit who may never come back to me again." The accompanying picture showed him boarding a plane, his face grief-stricken, as if he had recently lost the love of his life in some great tragedy. She became even more contemptuous when the next picture showed him at a piano in his luxurious California beach house, working on sheets of music propped up on the piano. "I am dedicating the theme music to her. *Remember Yesterday* will be premiering soon in Minneapolis. I hope everyone who sees it will understand what it's like to lose the one you love."

Drivel! Pure drivel! But what a fantastic publicity stunt to promote Patricia Blake's movie. She was positive the public would fight for tickets to attend the opening of a movie in which Devlin Paige had dedicated the score to his lost love.

He had rearranged the facts to suit his own purposes and she was curious to learn how he had managed it. She walked to the phone booth at the corner of the store and called long-distance information. She got the number for the *Chronicle* and called Floyd Mattlock, the reporter who had received a punch in the jaw for his overenthusiastic approach to this story.

"Mr. Mattlock, this is Raine Morgan," she said when his voice came on the phone.

"Miss Morgan. How nice of you to follow up on our story. Mr. Paige was most generous and we were happy to help in the publicity for *Remember Yesterday*. None of us knew that parts of the movie had been filmed on the Blake property, some in that cabin where we found you. Honestly, we really didn't know." He sounded apologetic; Raine was more intrigued than ever. She didn't have to ask him leading questions, for Floyd Mattlock offered her more information than she had hoped to gain. She almost bit her tongue when he asked if Devlin had given her a tour of the Blake lodge. Her terse negative was ignored as the man talked on and on.

"I'm glad you understand, Mr. Mattlock," Raine said when he finally paused long enough for her to enter the conversation. "It was nice of your paper to cooperate."

Mattlock sounded like a conspirator as he laughed into the receiver. "Well, Devlin pointed out that this area would gain a lot of tourist attention when the Patricia Blake film is released. His explanation was so much more interesting than the truth, wasn't it?"

"Oh, indeed it was," Raine agreed, her mouth tight. She wondered exactly what Devlin had told him. She didn't even have to ask, for Floyd Mattlock was a most talkative sort.

"*Today's Woman* got the exclusive on Paige's contribution to the film, but we sold the best love story since *Romeo and Juliet*. Is the article on Paige coming out before the movie?"

"Article?" Raine breathed, then covered her lapse with a casual laugh. "I'm not sure, Mr. Mattlock."

"He's a shrewd operator," Mattlock laughed. "We'll all profit by his feel for good publicity. 'Course it's his business knowing what the public will buy. Wouldn't people laugh if they found out his 'beautiful spirit' was a lady reporter writing a story about his change of professions? How'd you hear about that, anyway?"

"Kept my ear to the ground," Raine replied, with the first cliché she could think of.

"Bet your editor loves you," Mattlock said, then told her he had to get off the phone. She thanked him for speaking with her and hung up.

In a daze, she dialed Sheila Hemmings and was amazed to learn that what Mattlock had told her was all true. Devlin had stopped at the *Today's Woman* offices on his way to Los Angeles the day after Raine had called in from the farm. The office was still in an uproar. Sheila hadn't called Raine to talk about it because, of course, she had assumed that Raine had been in on the plan from the beginning. Sheila congratulated her on her part in the fantasy Devlin developed for the newspapers and gossip magazines, and told her that her in-depth interview with Devlin Paige was set up for the following week. Sheila was ecstatic that *Today's Woman* would be the first granted an interview with Devlin about his retirement from the concert circuit and his concentration on composing. Devlin had relayed an invitation from Patricia Blake to Raine to stay at her lodge and attend the prepremiere party she was giving. He had graciously given his permission for Raine to accompany him and take as many pictures as she wanted. Devlin was due back in Minneapolis at the middle of the week and Raine could fly with him to northern Minnesota on his chartered plane. Raine hung up the phone in a state of shock.

Devlin was more devious than anyone she had ever met. It had taken him a few phone calls and a short visit to Sheila, and everything had been worked out to his satisfaction. The local newspapers had been bought off with a juicy story to sell nationally for the romantic public's enjoyment. *Today's Woman* had itself an exclusive and *Remember Yesterday* would get a lot of free publicity before its release. Her mishap on skis and the subsequent interlude with him had simply become a source of publicity for him, to be used to its best advantage. He had reduced the whole thing to a fairy-tale story that increased his popularity and added to his public image of a mysterious and highly romantic figure.

She wondered what he had told his famous friends about her. Had he described her as a nosy reporter who had readily fallen in with his publicity stunt, or had he told them that she had foolishly fallen in love with him and he could manipulate her in any way he chose? He must have explained away her presence in his life easily, for no one had bothered to seek her out. Before meeting him, she had thought he had gotten rich on his good looks instead of his talent. He had certainly proved that he was capable of more devious methods to attain success. What woman could resist a story about a man falling hopelessly in love with a spirit woman whose memory haunted him and inspired him to write beautiful music.

Since the picture was due to be released soon, she angrily realized that the music must have been composed long ago. He had not gone to the cabin to write music as she had believed, but had probably gone there to relax for a couple of days. Running over the location of the cabin in her mind, then considering the likelihood of a citified man like Devlin hiding out in such a totally isolated spot, Raine's brow drew together. I'll just bet that cabin was remote! She had probably stayed those two days with Devlin Paige when the Blake lodge—complete with telephone, no doubt—was a short distance away. The thought made her blood boil. He had made a total fool of her! He only wanted to keep me there to get me into bed, she seethed.

How could she have been so naive as to have believed anything he said? Lying came as easily and convincingly to his lips as the lyrics for his songs! His only saving grace was that she had been granted the interview set for next week and it would be a plum for her career. Grudgingly, she admitted she should be grateful to him for the interview and for keeping her name out of the papers. However, she was still insulted at the thought of his taking advantage of her gullibility and was still steaming on Monday morning when she took the bus back to Minneapolis. She went straight to her office and was immediately cornered by Sheila.

"You are a sly fox, Raine, dear." Sheila gave her a hug. "Guess who called me this morning?"

"Who?" Raine hid her confusion by taking her seat behind her desk.

"Patricia Blake. She was sorry she didn't get to meet you up north last week, but wants you to come for the party she's holding at her lodge for the movie crew. You realize the script for *Remember Yesterday* is based on her memoirs. The story is about her girlhood, when her father owned a logging camp up north. I'm sure you know that the cabin where you located Devlin Paige was a prop built for the movie set exactly how Patricia remembered it...."

A prop? The cabin had been nothing but a prop? Raine wished she had Devlin's face in front of her so she could blacken both of his attractive hazel eyes. Why hadn't she remembered all of the articles she had read about the Blake-Rettering romance and how Patricia's roots had always been in Minnesota? The woman's story was well known, but Raine hadn't been able to think past Devlin's presence the entire time she had been with him. She tried to concentrate on Sheila's enthusiastic monologue.

"The movie depicts Miss Blake's rise to stardom and the love she always had for Jacob Rettering, a lumberjack." It was all coming back to Raine now—now, when it was too late to do her any good. Patricia Blake, the prima donna of the Metropolitan Opera, must have been staying within shouting distance the entire time Raine had spent with Devlin. Why, he probably could have taken me to the main lodge any time he chose! she thought. Was there no end to Devlin's deviousness?

Sheila caught her attention again by waving an old clipping from a past edition of *Today's Woman*. "This will be priceless when we print the story."

Raine looked at the familiar face of Patricia Blake, ageless and beautiful as she stood in a full-length white coat before a lofty spruce tree. A tall, ruddy-faced man with silver hair stood next to her, and between them was a large German shepherd with a very familiar-looking black muzzle. "Nice dog," Raine said as her stomach plummeted to the ground with an angry jolt.

"Miss Blake married her lumberjack a few years ago. As the story goes, Wolfe—that's the dog—was instrumental in getting them back together again. Devlin told me that Wolfe played the dog's role in the movie. Nice touch, don't you think? That dog now leads a pampered life in the Rettering home."

"Excuse me, Sheila." Raine couldn't listen to another word and almost ran to the door. "I really can't talk to you right now."

"Oh, dear," Sheila said as she came around the desk, but Raine had already escaped down the hall.

Four

"Miss Morgan." Devlin extended his hand in polite greeting as he faced Raine across the faded linoleum-blocked floor of the small airport.

"Mr. Paige," she returned, equally as smooth. "Let me introduce you to my photographer, Darryl Standish."

Darry moved forward to shake Devlin's hand. Raine thought she saw a slight tightening in the muscles along Devlin's jaw, but she decided she must have been mistaken when he began asking Darryl casual questions about his job. While the two men talked, Raine was able to survey Devlin. Dressed casually in a pair of rust-colored cords, with an off-white Irish fisherman's sweater showing beneath his rough tweed jacket, he was devastatingly attractive. His dark auburn hair gleamed richly beneath the overhead light, catching Raine's eyes as if she were a ship lost at sea homing in on a beacon. She had to make sure that this time she wouldn't be so bewitched by his virile lure as to let down her guard.

"Come meet the rest of my entourage." Devlin moved to take Raine's arm, but she quickly sidestepped and tucked her hand into Darryl's arm. She was certain her move took Devlin by surprise, for his mouth tightened ominously before he turned away and grinned at the group of people waiting to meet them near the coffee machine.

He introduced Raine and Darryl to the pilot and his agent, a short, stocky man named Ron Dunn. Ron gave Raine no more than a cursory nod from his balding head before Devlin presented a woman named Evelyn Smythe. Evelyn, a petite, middle-aged woman with steel gray hair, clasped Raine's hand and offered the condemning information that she had worked as Devlin's secretary for many years.

The smile of greeting froze on Raine's face and she glanced sidelong at Devlin. There was no mistaking his brief wince. Raine could not imagine this efficient-looking, smiling woman before her ever provocatively occupying Devlin's tub, waiting for him to succumb to her mature charms. Recovering from the momentary shock she had experienced at further proof of Devlin's deviousness, Raine asked, "Did you accompany Mr. Paige on location?"

"No, I stayed to complete the work in Los Angeles. He really didn't need the services of a secretary while he put the finishing touches on the score here in Minnesota." Evelyn had no idea she was digging the hole deeper for her boss. "This trip is my reward for keeping my nose to the grindstone."

"How kind of Mr. Paige," Raine mouthed insincerely, casting a killing glance at Evelyn's longtime employer. She was gratified that Devlin was feeling enough guilt over his deceit that he couldn't meet her eyes, quickly turning away when the pilot caught his attention.

"We can board now, Mr. Paige." The pilot pointed to the exit that led outside to where their small private plane was ready for take-off. Raine didn't wait more than a second to comply with the pilot's directions. Maneuvering herself in front of Darryl to avoid further contact with Devlin, she walked out the door and crossed the short expanse of tarmac to the plane. She stepped up on the wing to gain access to the inside. Before Darryl climbed up behind her, Raine heard Devlin's voice telling him that he should check to make sure his equipment was handled properly. Raine watched with dismay as Darryl hopped off the wing and went to speak to the pilot. Aware that there was no protest she could make gracefully, Raine glared at Devlin, who immediately took Darryl's place on the wing.

"Move on back, Miss Morgan." Devlin blocked the door with his body. "We'll take the double seat at the rear. It has a magnificent view out the back domed window."

Holding her spine ramrod straight, Raine edged to the back of the plane. When Devlin placed his hands on her shoulders, she tensed, and caught her breath as he smoothly assisted her in removing her chocolate suede jacket, hanging it in a small cupboard behind their seat. Knowing she was effectively trapped, Raine slid onto the blue velour-covered seat and nervously occupied herself with straightening her brown, split-seam straight skirt. She crossed her booted legs and edged as close to the wall of the plane as possible. The seat was barely wide enough for two people; and when Devlin sat down beside her, his face split in a devilish grin, she could feel the brush of his thigh against hers. Both of them knew it was deliberate as he waved innocently to Darryl. "You'll enjoy sitting up by the pilot. The view is much better from the second seat. You should be able to get some good aerial shots."

Raine sat in mute frustration as Darryl gave the thumbs-up signal and Evelyn and Ron positioned themselves in the two seats in front of her. It took the pilot only a few minutes to radio the tower, rev up the engines and prepare for takeoff. Raine rudely pushed Devlin's helpful hands aside and fastened her own seat belt, refusing to meet his eyes. She knew she wasn't handling this very well, but she didn't care. Being near Devlin was bad enough, but she couldn't bear for him to touch her. She turned her head to the window and kept her eyes firmly fixed on the runway outside.

A tiny thrill of excitement curled inside her stomach as the small plane lifted off the runway and rose in a slow arc, turning north. The skyline of Minneapolis rapidly became smaller as the plane gained altitude. The clustered skyscrapers dropped out of view, to be replaced by the black-and-white crisscross of snow-covered fields and tar-covered country roads. They were off the ground for almost fifteen minutes before Devlin decided to recapture her attention.

"We have to talk," he said, much too close to her ear. His soft breath on her neck made her jump and she sensed his knowing amusement. She glanced quickly to the seats ahead of them; but it was apparent that, because of the noise from the engine, any conversation between herself and Devlin would not be overheard by the plane's other occupants. Raine was a captive audience, with a window on one side of her, Devlin on the other and the back of Evelyn's seat touching her knees. "There's no place to run." He read her thoughts and she glared angrily at his satisfied grin. "I can explain..." he began.

"I think this whole incident is self-explanatory. I'm sure you're very pleased with yourself." She kept her voice low, concerned that by some quirk the others might hear. She didn't want a soul to realize she had been personally involved with Devlin.

"I kept your name out of the papers, didn't I?" he said, stung by the forbidding tone of her voice. "Don't you know what kind of publicity you would have been in for?"

She had simmered for days over that ridiculous story he had fed to the media. The dam of her anger broke and her ire burst through like a tidal wave. "You miserable...I could have been rescued two minutes after you found me," she accused. "The Rettering lodge is probably quite close to that cabin where you took me," she berated. "All I want to do is conduct this interview, write my story and get back to Minneapolis. I hope that when this weekend is over I'll never have to see you again."

His hazel eyes emitted sparks to match her own. "You little idiot! That cabin was over a mile from the lodge, and when I pulled you out of that river you were in no shape to be carried very far. We both could have died out there if I'd tried to get you all the way to the lodge in the middle of that blizzard. Besides, you were so wet and cold that I had to take care of you all night long. You were delirious half of the time, and when you finally warmed up and I knew you were going to be all right, I was too tired to even think about fighting my way a mile through the snow in the middle of the night. I was terrified from the minute I saw you break through the ice!"

"I've already thanked you for saving my life, but you could have taken me to the lodge the next day," she raged. "After all, I was well enough to go outside and play in the snow with you."

A slow smile teased across his face. "After playing with you I didn't want to take you anywhere. Besides," he shrugged his shoulders, "I would have lost my way within yards of the cabin. It was still snowing pretty hard. It was safer to stay where we were, and that's the truth!"

"The truth," she scoffed. "I'll concede the weather and maybe the distance between the cabin and the lodge, but there is little else you didn't lie about. Miss Smythe hardly seems the type to invite you into her bath. Or how about that miserable stray dog who happened by? Wolfe is a most beloved, pampered pet, as well as a movie star."

He nodded sagely, and she wanted to hit him. A thick wave of dark auburn hair fell over his brow and he brushed it aside. He dropped his hand and covered her cold fingers. She tried to pull out of his grasp but his hand merely tightened firmly.

"So I exaggerated things—but I did go to the cabin for a rest and I had to protect myself. How many reporters do you think have tried to get to me by pulling some kind of stunt, as I thought you had?" he asked reasonably.

"I'm sure I don't know and I don't care," she hissed, and again attempted to pull her hand away.

"I didn't dare trust you, Raine," he insisted, dropping his voice to a sensual level that made her heart contract. "For all I knew, you could have been there to get a story. News of my whereabouts could have leaked out and you might have been lying to me about your role at the magazine. You are a beautiful woman, and the temptation was almost overwhelming to tell you all about my changing career." He used his gorgeous eyes to convey his sincerity, probing her face for any sign of melting. He didn't find any. She had taken great pains to prepare for this confrontation and wasn't about to let him charm her into falling for yet another string of lies.

"Wasn't it pretty obvious that I'd ended up in that cabin by accident?" Raine demanded.

"I guess I knew that after the first few hours that morning, and I will be forever grateful to Mother Nature for giving me a perfect setup to get to know you better. After all, you said you didn't think very highly of me, and I took that as a direct challenge. The setting was unbeatable—we were alone in the world, just one man and one woman. I wanted time—time to prove that your estimation of me was wrong, to make you want me as much as I wanted you. I was enjoying your company too much to risk letting you in on the truth and spoil everything that was building between us."

Raine felt cold. He was monumentally egocentric—thinking only of his desires with never a care for her own feelings. Her mouth thinned and she averted her face, denying him even the slightest softening of understanding. She had wanted him—still wanted him—but Devlin

Paige desired her passion only on a physical level. She wanted far more from him and doubted that he was capable of giving it to her.

Sitting close to her, Devlin realized several things at once—she was terribly hurt, she was as beautiful as he had remembered and he was steadily losing ground. He shut his eyes momentarily to savor her sweet feminine scent that brought back a surge of memory. He had warmed her lovely body with the heat of his own and slept with her delicate fragrance claiming him, inch by inch. She was getting to him and his temper was near the boiling point. He wasn't used to having to explain himself. Most women let him handle everything with no questions, but this one—this one not only required explanations, but made him feel as though he had egotistically mishandled the entire episode. He was determined to crack through the defensive barrier she had erected against him, and his lips quirked upward. No understanding and welcoming smile for me, Raine? We shall see, Snow Maiden, we shall see, he said to himself. He allowed her to sulk for a few more minutes before he went on the attack again. He needed to see if she had shut down her reactions to him on all levels.

"I'm going to kiss you, Raine. I thought I would warn you before you made a fool of yourself by calling everyone's attention to us." He hid his enjoyment of her incredulous expression with difficulty as her wide brown eyes showed both anger and excitement. He reached over and placed one finger over her lips in silent warning. He focused on her enticing mouth, then stroked her lips apart with his finger. Finally, he leaned across the seat and turned her toward him.

Raine sat mutely, trying to strengthen herself against the effect of his nearness, with her internal sensors screaming alarms to her entire body. Her view was limited to the compelling liquid brandy of his eyes and the gold lights that ignited his pupils. "Don't," she whispered, but her breathlessness was more invitation than denial and he smiled, indulgently.

The taste of his mouth was thrillingly familiar, sapping her resistance as he stroked her tongue with enticing probes meant to incite her response. All thought was centered on the overpowering touch of his lips, she didn't realize that he meant to take more. His hand slid beneath her sweater and she was shot through with sensual warmth when his thumb flicked the hardness of her nipple. Electric shocks began in the pit of her stomach and met in the throbbing crests of her breasts as his hand claimed her fullness. His soft growl was a question and she answered it by giving in to temptation and touching him. Her fingers splayed in his hair. How she had longed to feel this way again! A soft whimper of acquiescence increased the seduction of his lips; and as her heart soared to the rhythm he demanded, he began slowly to bring her back to reality. His hand fell away from her breast and rested lightly on her waist; his lips pulled back from her mouth and lingered for a gentle caress of her cheek before he leaned back in his seat. His hands and lips were gone, but it was several moments before she could open her eyes.

"Spring thaws are so lovely," he teased tenderly, and her deep blush was added proof that she had melted further than he knew.

"Did you say something, Devlin?" Evelyn turned in her seat to smile back at them.

"Just discussing the pleasant weather we're having," he said, with aplomb, and Evelyn subsided back in her seat before Raine could remark on the knowing twinkle in the secretary's blue eyes when she spied Raine's flushed cheeks.

It took Raine several moments to control her ragged breathing and she was beginning to have trouble remembering that she was angry with Devlin. So what if he was a manipulative and totally unscrupulous man—he made her feel like the most desirable woman in the world.

"You used me." Raine made a valiant effort to rekindle her anger.

"In a way," he admitted, then continued, "but definitely not in the way I had hoped."

"Oh!" Raine was thrown completely off balance again. Devlin Paige was sexually intoxicating. "That . . . that story you told the papers was ridiculous. I don't know why anyone believed it."

"They believed it because I did a terrific job of acting. Didn't you see any of the pictures?"

"You bought off Floyd Mattlock," she accused, and he nodded.

"You were finished writing the music before I ever got there." He nodded again.

"You twisted everything to suit your own selfishness," she insisted.

"Guilty as charged, but if you accuse me of planning for Wolfe to arrive when he did, you'll be way off base. I could have strangled that mutt with my bare hands."

"I think we should forget that part." Raine squirmed uncomfortably in her seat, but knew he was well aware of the trend of her thoughts. He shrugged his shoulder and smiled the famous Devlin Paige smile.

"Now that we have all that squared away, let's discuss something more interesting."

"Like what?" she asked warily, unsure how he had managed to admit to his crimes without making her feel like preparing a guillotine for his personal use.

"How is your career moving along?"

"Swell, thanks to you." She wrinkled her nose in distaste and he felt a distinct urge to touch the sun-kissed freckles that sprinkled over the impertinent tilt.

"See, my suspicious Snow Maiden, all has worked out beautifully. If your name had been romantically linked with mine you would have had much more to be angry about. Reporters show no mercy and every curve of your sweet body would have been public domain.''

His words sparked an idea in Raine's mind. He had just given her the ammunition to illustrate her resistance to his charm. "I don't intend to show any mercy, either." His large brown eyes sparkled with pleasure as his brow rose. "Every line of that lean physique of yours will be public domain once I've written my story. I am one of those reporters you despise so much, remember?"

"What?" His disbelieving snort was so loud that Evelyn popped up over the seat to see what the excitement was all about.

"I'm missing an interesting conversation," Evelyn exclaimed. "Ron is snoring away like a buzz saw, which is worse than the noise from these engines. Are you beginning your interview already, Raine?"

"No, I'm only asking for Mr. Paige's vital statistics. Our readers will want that information so they can mentally match the pictures in the layout with the personal information in the article." Evelyn's laughter was loud and full of pure enjoyment.

"Now wait a minute..." Devlin was struggling with this unsuspected broadside, which had left him temporarily defenseless.

Raine took out her small recorder and thrust the microphone under Devlin's chin. She didn't tell him she hadn't put a tape in the machine. "Height, weight, chest size. We'd like to know what size pants you wear and the difference in your biceps when flexed or unflexed." Dark color swept up his cheeks as he glared first at her, then at his secretary. Evelyn gave a totally unsympathetic chuckle and slid down out of sight. Devlin thrust the microphone away from his face and looked as if he wanted to crush the small machine that was balanced on her knee. "You suggested this in-depth interview, didn't you?" Raine asked innocently, widening her eyes until her lashes brushed her upper lids.

Whereas seconds ago he had looked supremely arrogant and totally confident about her weakness where he was concerned, now he looked slightly confused and a bit wary. She kept a straight face as he narrowed his gaze on the mike she held casually in her hand. "Didn't you?" she prodded.

"Are you saying you were after an interview from the very beginning?" A bewilderment and increasing anger were in his voice. Raine took a deep breath to steady her nerves. If she didn't throw some obstacle in his path, he would ride roughshod over her emotions and take what she no longer could hold back.

"As you said, it all worked out beautifully." Raine threw caution to the winds and smiled widely. "I appreciate your keeping my name out of the papers. Now my by-line can appear on this interview with no scandal attached to threaten my credibility." She matched his previous tone when he had admitted to shamelessly manipulating the truth to suit himself. She felt her stomach knot from the force of his penetrating stare, which seemed to reach out and condemn her to some faraway darkness; and she thought she must have imagined the pain that appeared for a brief moment before his eyes glazed over to ice.

"I underestimated you, it won't happen again." The richness of his voice had lost its charm. "We'll wait until we reach the lodge before beginning our interview. I'm sure your photographer friend has seen enough of the

sights by now. I'll see if he wants to trade seats
and discuss the format with you.'' He got up
from the seat, keeping his head bent as he maneuvered his tall, powerful body gingerly toward the front of the plane. Raine shut her
eyes to block out the sight of the rigid set to his
wide shoulders and the unforgiving line of his
spine. She should have felt relieved that she
had just ruined any chance she had of becoming romantically involved with Devlin Paige.
Wasn't that what she had planned to have
happen? She had gotten her wish; so why did
she feel as if the bottom had dropped out of
her world and she was plummeting through
space with nothing to break the force of her
fall? She wasn't able to dwell on her misery
very long, as Darryl was quickly dispatched
back to her side.

"I can't see why women fall all over themselves to get to that guy." Darryl gave an exaggerated sigh. "Tell me what he's got that I
haven't."

Raine glanced over Darryl's figure as if ap-
praising it, saw the narrower shoulders and
slighter frame, the dark blond curly hair and
smooth pleasant face. No, he didn't emit the
potent signals Devlin did—signals that set

every nerve screaming in reaction. Darryl's presence was comfortable. "In many ways, Darryl, you are far more attractive than he." Raine spoke in an odd little voice that got Darryl's immediate attention.

"Don't tell me you've fallen for him like the rest of the female population?" He groaned at her burning cheeks. "Brother! How did he accomplish so much in so short a time? I've been trying to get to you for a year."

Raine was going to have to devise some method of hiding her emotions. If Darryl could read her face so easily, how long would it be before Devlin did the same? "I haven't fallen for him. He is a conceited, arrogant chauvinist with the most beautiful body I've ever seen."

"I'm going to enroll in a night course in weightlifting and rock-and-roll gyrations as soon as possible." Darryl made a wry face and reached for her hand. "Don't let him find out how you feel, Raine. Right now he thinks you're a smart lady reporter. Don't let him find out you came right off the farm and this is your first serious assignment."

She tried to look grateful for her friend's sage advice. She couldn't tell Darryl that Devlin knew exactly what she did at the magazine before she had met him. She wished she had asked Sheila if Devlin had asked any personal questions about her. Maybe he didn't yet know that she had led such a sheltered life and even now didn't live alone, but shared an apartment with a childhood friend. She had desperately tried to come off as an independent woman who knew the ins and outs of the journalism business, but if he knew her whole background he would realize it was all a huge bluff to defend herself against his single-minded approach. He was honest about wanting an affair with her—the glow in his sherry-colored eyes couldn't be contrived—but an affair with Devlin Paige would be disastrous. She couldn't let him find out more than she chose to tell him, and hoped he would disappear out of her life as soon as this interview was over. It would take her years to forget him as it was.

Five

A huge oak log splintered and cracked in the gigantic stone fireplace, shooting sparks across the glazed terra-cotta tiles of the raised hearth. Jacob Rettering jabbed at the offending log with a black iron poker and apologized to his guests. His rough-hewn face beneath a thick mane of silvered hair creased in a smile that highlighted the crinkled laugh lines besides his piercing gray eyes. "Hate to put a screen in front of a roaring fire, and I detest those glass doors so many folks are rigging up, but it might be best if we sat back a ways from the hearth. Wouldn't want anybody to get a hole burned in their clothes from a shooting spark. That log is mighty dry."

His wife gave him an indulgent smile and curled her tiny body closer beneath his arm. Patricia Blake looked as much at home in her wool slacks and hand-knit Nordic sweater as she did when on the stage at the Metropolitan Opera House clad in a shimmering formal gown. She had put everyone at ease as soon as they had arrived, personally escorting each guest to his room and making sure that he was comfortable. Dinner had been an informal affair eaten on trays around the large fireplace, which dominated one wall of the rough-timbered, cathedral-ceilinged main room.

"No one makes a pot of chili like you, Pat." Devlin spoke from his comfortable position on a brown leather chair. His long legs were stretched out before him and his feet were resting on a hassock. He looked completely at home and was on a warmly familiar basis with both his host and hostess. He accepted a large snifter of brandy from the hands of a sultry-looking brunette in tight, shiny pants and a deep, V-necked, white fuzzy sweater. The voluptuous woman sank, catlike, to her knees

beside his chair and placed a possessive hand
on his outstretched thigh.

Raine watched the brunette start a slow caress up the tight seam along Devlin's jeans and
her throat tightened painfully. So this was
Gisela Gariani, the Italian femme fatale who
was playing the supporting-actress role in *Remember Yesterday*. She was the only member
of the cast who had arrived early for tomorrow's party. She would be spending tonight at
the lodge.

"I've missed you, darling," Gisela's ac-
cented, throaty voice purred. She gazed ador-
ingly up at Devlin's face, watching him take a
sip of brandy, and moistened her pouting red
lips as his mouth touched the rim of the crys-
tal.

"Thanks. I wrapped up my end of things in
L.A. So all that remains for us to do is wait for
the opening. Glad I didn't have more to do
than write the score. I don't envy those guys
who had to put it all together." He moved his
leg slightly away from the fingers that were
moving steadily upward on his thigh. Raine
could have laughed when he abruptly got up
from the chair and moved across the room to
sit down on the hearth. His expression was

annoyed and she could appreciate how he must feel being stalked by the opposite sex so relentlessly. Gisela had not let up on him since their arrival and now Raine could see that Devlin regarded her as a pest. Gisela had a seductive voice and a figure to match, but Devlin made no bones about his aversion to the predatory glimmer in her feline eyes. Raine hid her grin, appreciating this role reversal. Devlin was being sexually harassed on the job and didn't seem to be handling it much better than Raine would have if she had been the object of such pawing. She felt no sympathy for him, for as far as she was concerned he had asked for it. Every performance he gave was an exhibition of his body. While his music and lyrics were beautiful, it was the husky quality of his voice and the suggestive gyrations of his body that made his concerts sellouts. Gisela had obviously fallen for his sex-symbol image and was treating him the way his image demanded. The woman refused to be put off so easily. Raine could not hide her smile of pure enjoyment when Gisela crossed the room and blithely placed her arm around Devlin's neck and wound one red polished nail in his hair.

Patricia was more sympathetic to Devlin's plight and rescued him by asking him to go outside and bring in more logs. The fire was positively roaring and there was an ample supply of fuel stacked in a large copper kettle next to the hearth; so Patricia didn't fool anyone with her ploy. Gisela gave a disappointed sigh, but then volunteered to accompany him. Devlin looked desperate. This time it was Jacob who came to his rescue, inserting, "No reason for you to chill yourself out there, signorina. This is man's work. Dev and I will weather the elements, you just stay warm by the fire."

The look on Devlin's face was nothing short of undying gratitude as he quickly donned his jacket and practically bolted to the door.

Devlin's absence from the room brought Darryl to Gisela's side like a shot. A few blatant compliments and the vibrant Italian switched allegiance without any sign of a struggle. In a few more moments, the twosome drifted out of the room, arm in arm. Darryl threw Raine a lascivious grin over his shoulder as he passed her with his prize.

"You look tired, Ron. It's been a long day for all of us and I for one am ready to call it a night." Evelyn pulled the sleepy middle-aged man from his half-reclining position on the couch. They said their good-nights and disappeared up the massive oak staircase to a wide balcony that surrounded the large room.

Patricia waited until she heard the closing of their doors off the balcony before coming to sit beside Raine. With a twinkle in her eye, she commented, "Do you think it's safe to ring the 'all clear' signal for Devlin? I believe the poor boy is safe from his attacker for the remainder of the night. If I'm correct, your photographer friend is thoroughly enjoying his role as stand-in."

Raine had not thought Darryl capable of such tomcat behavior. In the months she had gone out with him he had barely touched her. Her disapproval must have been clearly apparent on her expressive face, for Patricia chuckled. "It happens, my dear. When I was just beginning my career, there were women who found success far faster than I did by employing the very same methods as our Gisela. That's probably why she played her part in the film so well. We knew at the first reading that she was perfect. It was definitely typecasting.

"Devlin, on the other hand, can't seem to reconcile himself with his commercial image. He is two different people."

"Oh, he knows very well what effect he has on women," Raine couldn't help saying. "He's made a fortune because of it. His voice is certainly no calling card. His fans don't hear a note of his off-key singing once his body begins moving to the beat."

Patricia laughed at Raine's tone of disgust and Raine found herself joining in. "I have no sympathy for him if he finds himself being pawed by every woman who can get her hands on him."

"And wouldn't you like to be one of those women?" Patricia probed intuitively.

"I wouldn't stand a chance with him if I behaved like the other women in his life." Raine didn't understand how this conversation had gotten on such a personal level so quickly. For some reason she felt an instant affinity with Patricia Blake, and sensed it was returned. She had just revealed her most intimate thoughts and the woman honed right in on them.

"You want a chance with him, don't you, Raine?"

Confusion and extreme embarrassment showed in Raine's expressive eyes. "I don't know," she blurted miserably. She got up from the couch and went to stare into the fire, jamming her agitated hands into the back pockets of her brown cords. She was still standing there asking silent questions of the fire when Jacob and Devlin came through the door, each carrying a load of freshly split wood. Raine was unaware of the unspoken messages that passed between Jacob and Patricia, and of their exit. Several moments of silence passed before she turned around to find that they were gone. Devlin stood inches away from her, waiting patiently for her attention.

"Shall we start our 'in-depth' personal interview with the vital statistics you mentioned?" He took hold of her by both wrists and placed them behind her back, locking them there with one hand. Totally disconcerted, she arched away; but his other hand splayed across her back and jerked her to his chest. "Hmm...." He seemed to be concentrating. "I'd say you're about a thirty-six. What's your estimation of me?"

All breath left her body. She wasn't prepared for this blatant assault. "I don't think you really want the answer to that,'' she cautioned sarcastically, but he tightened his hold even more. His eyes glittered angrily and she realized the torment had only begun. He moved her hands down to his waist and guided them from front to back. ''Waist size?'' he prompted, then estimated for her. ''I think it's about thirty-three or thirty-four. Somewhere in there.'' He completely ignored her increasingly indignant struggles to get out of his embrace.

''Stop it!'' she demanded, trying to pull her hands away as he moved them from his waist to his hips. She could feel the curve of his thigh bones beneath the tight Levi's. Her fingers began to burn with sensation as he moved his hips suggestively. Her lashes dropped to cover her reaction to him and his dry laugh was no inducement to open them again when all she would see was his mocking enjoyment of the situation.

''Your tactile perception must be more acute than your visual,'' he jeered. ''We'll move on then, shall we?''

His hand came to the nape of her neck and twisted in her hair, forcing her head back as he bent his face down to hers and his mouth opened over her lips. As his tongue ruthlessly explored her mouth, his hand guided hers across and down his tautly muscled torso until she had far more information about his hard male contours than she wanted.

Breathing raggedly, she realized she was trembling. The exultant sound he made was muffled by his possessive kiss and her mortification increased to compete with the fierce hunger she could no longer hide. Her full breasts were hard points probing his chest. A liquid warmth spread from limbs that suddenly refused to support her. He let her sink and followed her down on the tawny deep-piled hearth rug, trapping her hands between their bodies. His muscular thighs held her captive, straddling her hips. His mouth continued to explore hers while his hands made short work of unbuttoning her blouse. He released the front clasp of her bra with an expert flick of his thumb and forefinger, and her softness was released to fill his hands. He palmed her breasts; then his fingers began lightly brushing their tips until both nipples were straining for his caress. She writhed beneath him, consumed with need as his lips trailed down her throat and flirted with the swollen tips, circling, enticing and finally taking one inside his mouth. He suckled gently and her back arched in response. Her hands pressed hungrily against him and their frenzied movement brought a fierce growl from deep within his chest. He pulled away from her and stood up, staring down at her with eyes that burned like those of a marauding lion.

"If you require more information about my statistics for your interview, I'll be upstairs. Patricia placed us next door to one another."

Raine lay sprawled upon the rug in a state of shock. Quivering with reaction to his deliberate arousal of her and the cold-blooded rejection that followed, she watched with stunned eyes as he turned his back and mounted the stairs. She had been given ample proof of his desire and yet he had turned off his response like an unfeeling machine. He was crude and despicable!

Slowly, she adjusted her clothing and tried to push away the thought that she had surrendered too quickly to the enticement of his body and the seduction of his lovemaking. She felt incapable of walking up the stairs, but managed to make it to the liquor cabinet in the corner and pour herself a stout measure of bourbon. She drank it straight. The undiluted liquor burned all the way down and was a welcome relief to the agony clutching her constricted throat. She would never forgive him for what he had just done to her! Never!

She was so distracted that she almost missed hearing the persistent scratching on the thick oak door. She crossed the room like a zombie and lifted the heavy latch to admit Wolfe. He lunged welcomingly upon her, licking the tears from her face, then sitting down on his haunches to stare up at her in silent inquiry. It was as if he understood that he had come too late to save her as he had done once before. He trotted obediently behind her as she replaced her glass on the bar and mounted the stairs.

Barely inside her room, she jumped, startled, and leaned forcibly against the door when she heard footsteps in the hall outside her room. She hurriedly slipped the lock in place and a moment later the knob turned. Wolfe emitted a low growl, and she heard a muffled oath before the steps receded and she heard the door of the next room open and close. Had Devlin come to finish what he had started? She didn't know if she could face him in the morning, let alone again tonight. She was satisfied he wouldn't be coming back when Wolfe bounded for her bed and settled himself on the down-filled comforter. Ignoring the cold chills that gripped her, she stripped off her clothes and pulled on a long flannel gown. She crept between the smooth sheets, shivering, her feet like ice. Thankful for Wolfe's presence, she slipped her feet beneath his warm weight and stared at the ceiling. Her ears tuned in to the restless pacing of the man in the next room and she lay awake for hours.

On the other side of the wall, Devlin strode to the door and reached for the knob, then paused and jammed his hands into his jeans. He went back to the window and gazed out into the star-studded night. He had known instantly that Raine was coming up the stairs, but she had locked her door against him a moment before he reached it. She had made him so angry on the flight to the lodge that he had been ready to throttle her. Up until she had confessed she had been after an interview with him all along, he had judged her an innocent and beautiful woman—and one of the most honest ones he had ever met. Their day in the snow was a warm memory that he couldn't seem to erase from his mind. Could that same laughing Snow Maiden be the conniving reporter who would compromise herself for a story? Somehow her behavior today didn't ring true with everything he knew about her in the cabin. When he thought about the lengths he had taken to protect her reputation, he felt sick. Had he finagled and manipulated the newspapers to save a woman who knew the score far better than he? Tonight she had all but laughed at his predicament with Gisela and he had seen red. He had taken her up on her insistence to report his vital satatistics in a way she couldn't possibly have anticipated, but it had given him little pleasure. At first her shock had been a perfect revenge; but when he felt her hesitance in a situation where an experienced woman would have known exactly what to do, he began wondering if he had misjudged her. If she really were willing to go to any lengths to get a story, she would be in his bed right now, rather than safely behind a locked door in the next room.

Also, he mused, her relationship with Darryl Standish seemed nothing more than friendship. He remembered that she had denied ever having gone to bed with Darryl when he had interrogated her that first day. He had antagonized her frequently since then and wondered if the sudden change in her attitude was really her way to throw up some kind of defense. Was that possible? He didn't trust many women—couldn't afford to for self-preservation's sake—but he wanted desperately to trust Raine. When she had turned traitor in the plane it had come as a severe shock. Tonight he had ruthlessly reacted, and only now did he consider that he may have been way off base. If she were innocent of any deception, he had successfully ruined everything between them. On that note he got undressed and went to bed, but did not sleep any better than the woman in the next room.

Raine didn't make it downstairs for breakfast until late in the morning. The first thing she did was make sure that Devlin was not in the dining room before she joined her hosts and Evelyn. She was greeted with the smell of freshly brewed coffee and hot cinnamon rolls as she took her place.

"Didn't you sleep well, dear?" Patricia asked.

Raine knew that the dark shadows beneath her eyes had not been effectively camouflaged by her foundation makeup, but she had hoped her sleepless night would not be apparent. "I guess I'm too used to sleeping in my own bed. I'm sure I'll make up for it tonight." Her trite excuse was not bought by anyone.

"Devlin didn't look much better." Jacob gave her a kindly look from beneath his silvery brow. Raine swallowed and concentrated on her pastry. She could feel all eyes on her and began to squirm. She looked from one to the other and found they were all looking at her, encouraging her to confide in them. What did they suspect was going on between her and Devlin? They obviously had no idea that they were farther apart than the North and South Poles.

Patricia reached across the table and squeezed Raine's hand. "I bet you're thinking that you have walked into some kind of conspiracy." Both Evelyn and Jacob smiled reassuringly. "You see, Raine, all of us have loved Devlin for many years. When he came to us and told us about the beautiful woman he had just met, we thought at first it was only a passing fancy. Then we noticed the way he went about protecting your name from the news hounds—he did everything humanly possible to direct their attention elsewhere.

Frankly, that came as a surprise. He doesn't usually put himself out for people he doesn't already know well.

"We may not look like much of a family, but that's how we think about Dev. He never had anybody to care for him except us. He came off the streets of New York with a gigantic chip on his shoulder, but his lyrics would have made a grown man cry. His life consisted of moving from one foster home to another, and when he earned a grant to the Juillard School of Music it was like release from prison. Later he was discovered by a talent scout when he was singing in a rock group to supplement his grant. He was signed by Bryer Records. They've been exploiting his looks and personality with a lot of media hype to sell records. Last year he finally realized that the loyalty he had given to Bryer was destroying him from the inside out. We encouraged him to break his contract and start doing what he's always wanted to do—write music. He didn't publicly admit his decision until two weeks ago.... Don't you find that revealing?"

Raine had listened to Patricia's words with a mixture of emotions, each running turbulently across her face as Devlin's background and subsequent rise to fame was described. She had never thought about the possibility that Devlin was not free to act as himself. She didn't know what to say or what these people expected her to do about the information they had given her. "Why do you suggest that this has something to do with me?"

"Devlin told us it did," Patricia answered smoothly. "He said you had called him all the things he called himself and it sounded much worse coming from you. He has a fierce loyalty toward his agent, Ron, but when you told him he was wasting his talent and that you thought he was doing a disservice to the public by continuing to sell records by promoting his image rather than good music, he made up his mind to break his contract. Ron came here to talk Devlin out of it, but this time he's fighting a losing battle."

Raine's brown eyes widened and her brows rose with surprise. "Devlin has tried to get out of his contract before?"

"Many times," Patricia confirmed. "But always before, Ron made him believe that he would be hurting the very fans who had made him a success. This time, I think he is sure about leaving. The score for *Remember Yes-*

terday is really beautiful. In the end the public will gain if Devlin is allowed to write instead of sing. I think Ron realizes that because he left for L.A. not long after Devlin went out this morning.''

"I . . .'' Raine was astounded at these revelations. "He was very angry with me last night...and...he...'' She could not tell these people what Devlin had done to her the night before. It seemed she didn't have to, for Jacob started nodding his heavy head like an old philosopher.

"I knew you were in for it when Devlin caught you grinning at him over Gisela. He chopped wood outside until I got blisters just watching. You'd best be a mite kinder to him in the future, Raine. We are full up with fuel for the winter and I don't enjoy freezing my old bones in the cold to make sure Dev takes his temper out on something inanimate.''

"There's a lot more to it than Miss Gariani.'' Raine didn't know why she was explaining so much to these people who were practically strangers. She supposed it was the way they were talking to her about Devlin. She felt as though Jacob and Patricia were Devlin's parents and Evelyn a kindly aunt or older sister. She knew they were thinking of her as Devlin's latest love interest... or something more serious than that. ...How could they think that? She had not known Devlin long enough and, besides, he had proved last night that he held her in contempt. He might desire her body, but these people were mistaken if they believed she meant more to him than his other women. She had to set them straight. She liked them all too much to have them operating under the misguided impression that she meant something to Devlin other than a desirable woman he wanted to get into his bed.

"I'm only here to do a story on him," she insisted, watching the varying degrees of surprise on their faces. She continued, unable to stop saying what she felt they had to hear. "Devlin might not have liked what I said about him. He might even have allowed my opinion to finalize a decision he had already come to, but I must tell you there is nothing personal going on between us. He considers me a rather nosy journalist whose only interest in him is the story I can get for my magazine."

She didn't stay to see the reaction she got from her speech, but stood up abruptly from the table and walked swiftly out of the room.

She meant to go up to her bedroom, but decided a long walk would serve her better. She took her ski jacket and boots from the wall rack in front of the main door and went outside.

The Blake-Rettering property was rustically beautiful. She began walking down the graveled drive lined on each side by lofty firs, laden with heavy snow. She breathed in the crisp cold air, which was filled with the heady aroma of pine. Her boots crunched on the packed snow as she chose a track that led off the drive and into the woods, instinctively knowing what she would discover a mile down the steep path between the trees. As she walked on and on, a deep silence fell over the woods and she was alone with nature on her own bleak thoughts. Even now, on a sunny winter day, the trail was difficult to follow, and she had to admit that in a storm it would have been impossible.

The cabin looked exactly as it had when she had left it. She walked the few remaining yards to the door, trying not to look at the place where she had lain under Devlin in a bed of snow. She fought a losing battle with herself and retraced her steps. Wind had softened the clear imprint of their figures, but she could still make out the indentation of each of their figures. Moisture gathered in her eyes and she turned away. The interlude had only been part of a wintertime dream. She was surprised to find the cabin unlocked. She pushed open the door and entered. The clothesline no longer hung before the fireplace, but the large bed where Devlin had held her naked in his arms still occupied most of the room. She realized that the furnishings had really been props for the movie, for most of them had been packed inside large wooden crates marked "Olympia Productions." Just like the interlocking impression their bodies had left in the snow outside, the homey cabin had only been an illusion.

Six

Frowning in contemplation, Raine surveyed the clothes she had brought with her, which were neatly hung in a small knotty pine closet. Patricia had told her that tonight's gathering would be informal; so the velvet skirt and brocade top she had intended to wear seemed too dressy for the occasion. She finally decided on a soft, pink wool floor-length sweater dress that buttoned from the V neck to just below the knee. She placed her feet into deep rose suede pumps and fastened a heavy gold bracelet around her wrist. Chunky gold loops dangled from her ears and flashed whenever she moved her head. She wore her hair loose around her shoulders, falling in honey gold waves. A touch of mauve eye shadow, mascara on her long thick lashes and pink lip gloss completed her makeup. She dabbed her favorite scent at her throat and decided she was ready to join the party downstairs.

Evelyn joined her on the balcony and they descended the staircase together. Evelyn took Raine's arm in an affectionate gesture, making her feel as if she belonged with the group gathered below. Raine had not seen Devlin all day. He had disappeared from the lodge before she had come down for breakfast and as far as she knew hadn't returned all afternoon. When they paused momentarily at the top of the stairs, Raine scanned the crowd and was relieved when she didn't spy Devlin's dark burnished head. She didn't know if she could face him again and was glad that there would be so many people present tonight that it would be difficult to find themselves alone together.

She followed Evelyn to a group of newcomers to the lodge and was introduced to several members of the cast from *Remember Yester-*

day. That they had taken the time to attend was a glowing tribute to Patricia's popularity. Raine heard one man tease Patricia, telling her he wouldn't have interrupted his busy schedule for anyone but her—and a good day of skiing.

They were a friendly bunch, exchanging small talk and jokes but easily including Raine in their conversation. She found that movie people were not so very different from anyone else attending a party. Some looked bored, some seemed to enjoy every minute, and some fell in between. She made mental notes of those people who might be able to relay the most information about Devlin and his music.

The director, Dean Farringer, was well known in the business and his movies were always popular at the box office. His shiny bald head and sunny features brought smiles to the others whenever he spoke. They all seemed to respect him and Raine was sure that the movie crew had enjoyed working with him throughout the filming. She listened avidly to their reminiscences about *Remember Yesterday,* laughing at the difficulties they described in filming during a snowstorm and the hardships of moving their equipment through the deep drifts.

The woman who had played Patricia Blake in the movie was a well-known actress that Raine had always admired but never thought to meet. Vivian Randolph not only looked very much like Patricia, but was as warm and friendly. Raine thought Vivian's part had been yet another case of typecasting when she saw the two women together. Actress and opera star could have been sisters and seemed to thoroughly enjoy each other's company.

Raine accepted a delicious hors d'oeuvre from one of the white-coated caterers. She smiled across the crowded room at Darryl, who was unobtrusively circulating, taking candid shots. Even though she had a good memory, Raine jotted notes on a small pad throughout her conversations, keeping track of the fascinating details that would be of interest to her readers. She showed nothing but professional interest when Devlin's name was mentioned, smiling and nodding as she listened to several people praise his ability. According to them, his music had set the mood for the script. They had all heard the score before playing their roles, and had been moved by the poignant music.

Jacob's role had been taken by Kirk Summers, a roguish male actor who had a tremendous following. He was making the most of his time at the party by flirting with Gisela. The young Italian actress was obviously flattered and clung to Kirk's tall form like a climbing red rose.

Raine almost laughed as Darryl snapped a picture of Gisela gazing starry-eyed into Kirk's handsome face. Raine herself was fascinated by Kirk's countenance; and if she didn't think she would have seemed like some moony teenager, she would have asked him for his autograph.

Patricia had arranged for a small combo to play dance music. The musicians were set up around the concert grand piano and several couples drifted away from the conversations by the fire to begin dancing to the slow music.

"Here we are rubbing shoulders with the rich and the famous," Darryl remarked wryly as he came up to Raine and offered her one of the steaming mugs he held in his hand.

"Hot buttered rum," he answered her questioning look.

She took a sip of the rich cinnamon-tasting drink and licked the hot spice from her upper lip. "I hope you have gotten some good pictures," she said, then couldn't resist teasing Darryl about his night with Gisela. "I think you have done more than rub shoulders with some of these people."

Darryl's brow crinkled momentarily beneath his curly blond hair, before a boyish grin spread across his face. He shrugged his shoulders. "Had to make the most of my opportunities. See how quickly they pass?" he nodded toward the raven-haired beauty who was draped on Kirk Summers's arm.

"Where is the subject of our interview?" Darryl surveyed the crowded room with discerning blue eyes. "The women haven't formed giggling clusters anywhere, so Devlin must not have put in his appearance yet."

Raine frowned at that, disturbed that everyone—men and women alike—thought of Devlin as a sex symbol who drew women to him like flies. Didn't anyone sense what Devlin was like beneath the dynamic masculine exterior? She decided to pose the question, wondering if Darryl appreciated how shallow he had made Devlin sound. "Wouldn't you get tired of being the object of that kind of attention all the time? Don't you think it might get boring—these constant parties and interviews, adoring fans and investigations into your private life?''

''I'd love it.'' Darryl didn't take her seriously. ''Imagine walking into a room and having women swarm all over you like bees. I would be in my glory.''

The lusty glimmer in his eye made Raine laugh, but she still tried to get her point across. ''Come on, Darryl. Think about it from Devlin's point of view. He's hounded wherever he goes, he never has any privacy. I think it would be horrible to live in a glass house where even your body was considered the property of an adoring public.''

''Still stuck in the same rut, Raine?'' Devlin questioned angrily from behind her, missing all but the last line of her conversation. ''However much you may think otherwise, my body does not belong to my public and I'm getting a little tired of hearing it from you.''

''I didn't say—'' Raine began, but Devlin didn't allow her to complete her sentence. Darryl took one look at the dangerous glint in Devlin's eyes and picked up on the unspoken command for him to leave them alone. He gave Raine a sympathetic glance before he went to seek out a curvy redhead he had seen lingering by the bar.

"Come on. We're going someplace where we can talk without an audience," Devlin commanded. Raine had no choice but to accompany him as he dragged her along in his wake. Reaching the entryway, he grabbed a sheepskin jacket and a full-length hooded sable coat from the closet by the front door. He draped the coat around Raine's shoulders as he swiftly ushered her outside the lodge.

"I can't wear this! It doesn't belong to me," she protested, her brain just beginning to function after his high-handed tactics.

"Believe me, the owner won't mind." The grim set to his jaw and the challenging light in his eyes convinced her that any further protest would be useless. Besides, she couldn't help but appreciate the luxurious feel of the exquisite coat. The satin lining caressed her skin and her fingers reveled in the soft fur. She had never worn anything a fraction as expensive as the beautiful coat Devlin had thrown so casually over her shoulders. To her further surprise, he motioned her to a sleigh waiting a few yards away across the drive. "Get in!"

Suddenly afraid, Raine turned and took a step back toward the door. His dangerous tone and the ruthless set of his chin boded ill. She didn't want to be alone with him, especially after last night. The sleigh looked like something straight out of Dickens and under any other circumstances, Raine would have been enchanted. It was drawn by a sleek black horse who stood impatiently pawing the frozen ground; every time the animal tossed his gaily harnessed head, little bells would tinkle.

Before she could stop him, Devlin scooped her up and deposited her on the deep, recessed upholstered seat, then placed a heavy woolen throw across her lap. He carefully tucked it under her feet while she sat in mutinous silence, then unhitched the horse and climbed in beside her. A slight snap of the thick leather rein and the horse took off at a gentle trot.

The silver runners skimmed over the crusted snow. Neither of them spoke, the stillness of the hushed forest broken only by the shush of the runners along the icy ground and the occasional tinkling of bells attached to the horse's harness. To Raine it was a magical setting marred only by the brooding figure seated beside her. His hands, encased in leather gloves, were clenched on the reins and his silence was a threat. She dreaded whatever was coming, recalling the previous night in excruciating detail.

Devlin drew the sleigh to a halt in a secluded clearing surrounded by towering spruce and stately verdant firs. He fastened the reins to a brass ring on the sleigh and leaned against the upholstery to stare up at the sliver of silver moon that shone through the trees. His voice when it came was low and contained a note of harshness. "About last night—"

"I don't want to talk about last night, Mr. Paige!" Raine stated emphatically. "Take me back to the lodge. I don't want to be alone with you ever again."

She was not going to take any more from him without fighting back and certainly didn't want to listen to any more recriminations.

His arm slid around her shoulder and she cringed away. There was no mistaking his wince, but he had only intended to flip the hood of the coat over her hair. As if by his order, huge fluffy flakes of snow began sifting from the sky, glistening in the silver moonlight as they feathered to the ground. "What I did to you last night was unforgivable. I'm sorry." The harshness was gone and in its place a soft note of apology. She glanced quickly and caught his tentative expression, which deepened the grooves beside his mouth and softened the line of his jaw.

"You are?" She couldn't have been more surprised.

"I assumed—I realize, wrongly—that any woman who had done what I believed you did in order to get a story would have enjoyed gathering my statistics firsthand. Don't you see, Raine? I have had to condition myself to be constantly on guard for ulterior motives— especially with reporters—and when you told me you were after a story all along, I went into a tailspin. I knew you were different, but that hard-nosed reporter act you put on hit a nerve, dead center. It wasn't until I touched you, treated you like..." He swallowed some obstruction in his throat. "I've ruined it, haven't I? I wanted to apologize last night but I knew you wouldn't let me into your room."

"No matter how angry you were, you had no right to manhandle me as you did," Raine asserted quietly, wanting to succumb to the heartrending harshness in his voice, desperately hoping he wasn't explaining his actions to her only because his gigantic ego couldn't tolerate her rejection. "You weren't considering my feelings—only your dented male pride."

"It wasn't pride. I was really angry when I thought you were just like all the rest. I thought you had made a fool of me, but I see now that you just didn't trust me. Tonight I was prepared to go down on my knees, but you weren't exactly singing my praises to that photographer friend of yours." Bitterness narrowed his eyes. "What will it take to convince you I'm different from my public image?"

She realized then that his hurt went far deeper than she had thought. "You misunderstood what you heard me saying to Darryl." She had his immediate attention and was amazed that her opinion of him seemed to matter so much. "I was telling him how difficult it must be for you, having your life constantly dissected for public scrutiny." She tried valiantly to lighten the moment. "Why, you even believed the public wanted to know what you ate! It must be awful coping with that kind of thing all the time."

His smile was tight, but it was still a smile. "I can think of better terms to use to describe it."

She could feel some of her tension slowly draining away. Did she dare trust him? She huddled herself deeper into the richness of the luxurious coat, rubbing her cheek against the soft fur hood framing her face. "Of course, owning things like this coat wouldn't be too hard to get used to. You threw this at me as if it were some castoff meant for the Salvation Army."

That brought a grin, and her laughter joined his. When it died, they sat without touching in an awkward silence until Raine began to chatter nervously.

"I used to go on hayrides during the winter. It's been years since I've been out like this." She described those long-ago days when she had ridden in the back of a hayrack with a bunch of her friends, laughing and singing as they tumbled each other off the rack and onto the snow-covered fields of her parents' farm.

"They didn't have hayrides where I came from. I've done lots of things for the first time since meeting you." He glanced pointedly at the horse.

"You've never driven a sleigh?" She sat up straighter, searching his face and unable to keep her expression serious as he grinned unrepentantly.

"I got us this far without trouble, didn't I?" he pointed out reasonably.

"You acted like you'd done this a million times before," she accused, then gave the large black horse a dubious look. "This must be one of those horses who knows the property so well he doesn't need an experienced driver to guide him. I hope he knows his way back."

"I don't." He reached for her and tenderly pulled her against him, using his gloved hand to lift up her chin. "I've been trying to get you alone for what seems like an eternity. I've missed you, Raine. I want to...oh, God, I want to lose myself in you forever."

Wordlessly, they stared into each other's eyes. Raine saw a hunger, an aching need there had inspired an almost overwhelming response in her. She wanted to touch him, to reach out and smooth the sweep of dark flame hair from his forehead. She brought up her hand, not feeling the cold as her fingers touched his cheek.

Devlin blinked, spellbound by the soft, liquid brown eyes that were searching his face. When her fingers touched him, he was afraid she would soon draw back and he sat motionless. When the gentle hand moved down to explore the lean planes of his face with a tenderness he had not felt from a woman before, he groaned and pulled her closer, finding her soft mouth with his lips.

Under the black sky of a winter's night, in a glistening frosty glade, she was his and he kissed her deeply, soothing his craving for her. He drew warmth from her mouth and strength from her unbridled response. When their heavy coats became too much of a barrier, he gently pushed her back on the seat.

Raine watched him release the reins from the ring and start up the horse. She knew that his kiss had only begun what was building between them, and she wanted it to go on and on. She moved her head to rest on his shoulder, smoothing her cheek on the rough leather exterior of his sheepskin jacket as the sleigh slowly moved through the deep woods.

Raine knew instinctively where Devlin was headed, but not one word of protest passed through her lips. It was too late to turn back, for she realized she was in the only place she wanted to be—with Devlin.

He brought the sleigh to a halt outside the hewn-log cabin, which surprisingly welcomed their arrival by casting warm light upon their faces from its frost-laced windows. Devlin picked her up and carried her to the threshold, kicking open the door and ducking his dark head as they passed through.

A flickering crimson gold fire beckoned them; Raine didn't wonder how it had come to be there until later. Devlin lowered her in front of the glowing heat and tenderly removed her coat, once again treating it far too casually as he flung it away from them. "You show a total disregard for other people's property," she teased, as her fingers slid under his jacket and pulled it down his arms.

"I'm only concerned with my own," he murmured thickly, unbuttoning her sweater dress with trembling fingers. After he removed the lacy slip of her bra and gazed his fill of the soft curves revealed to him, he followed her down upon the deep pelt rug spread before the hearth. She realized vaguely that he must have planned the romantic accommodations, but nothing mattered to her as he brought his hands to her breasts and began molding the pearly flesh in his palms, thumbing her nipples with delicate skimming motions that made her tremble. "Beautiful... beautiful," he whispered as he shook his head and removed his hands only enough to jerk his sweater off over his head and remove his shirt.

She surrendered to the glorious feel of his body pressed against her, the rough, crisp hairs of his chest brushing her throbbing breasts and heightening her response. She wanted to touch him, could not wait to feel the entire length of his naked body with her hands. She struggled with the buckle of his pants, wanting no more barriers between them. He solved the problem himself, quickly unfastening his pants and pulling them and his white briefs down his long legs.

"Devlin," she moaned, as his hands began a tantalizing journey down her silken skin, caressing the smooth flesh over her hips and across her buttocks. His lips were at her breasts, licking the fevered curves until she trembled with need.

He answered her passionate rhythm to his touch with a tortured moan, sliding his body up beside hers as his mouth ignited her lips.

His tongue probed the deepest recesses of her mouth, greedily searching for the sweetness within.

Raine returned every hungry thrust, answering his searching tongue with explorations of her own, drinking in the taste of him. When his lips began nibbling along the fragile line of her jaw, then slipped to her throat and began pressing small kisses to the ultrasensitive skin, she clutched her fingers in his hair and murmured her pleasure. "Darling," she moaned as his hands stroked her smooth flesh, caressing her shapely legs and finally slipping between her thighs. His fingers were tuned to every delicate nerve ending, making her writhe with the pleasure of it.

"I want all of you, Raine," he mumbled thickly, shuddering as her fingers traced the line of dark hair down his chest to his stomach and beyond. When she found him, her name became an exultant cry wrenched from his throat. "I knew you would melt for me, Snow Maiden," he growled hoarsely, tantalizing her essence as she stroked his hair-roughened thighs, pleasing and enflaming him until his ragged breath was as tortured as hers. "This night you are mine."

Raine heard the muffled words and it was as if a cold shaft of air had swept over her body. She paused; this was one last opportunity for her to fend off the hot veils of desire he had wrapped around her senses. This night? What about all the nights after this one? She shivered, no longer completely warmed by the aroused masculine body that burned against her.

He had no doubt about how the evening would end, Raine fumed inwardly. He was so sure of me that he arranged this whole romantic setup from the sleigh ride to the fire. She had to know, had to find out if Devlin considered her just another conquest or if she was special to him. Did he love her? Forcing herself to ignore the play of his fingers upon her delicate skin, she twisted for space and murmured softly, "You planned this?"

He was kissing her, savoring her soft skin, and didn't sense the reason for her question, too far gone in passion to realize that Raine was no longer with him. "The wine, the fire, all my props won't be able to give me as much pleasure as you. Afterward we'll have champagne," he admitted huskily, moving his lips down her flat stomach. He grunted with astonishment when Raine forcefully pushed him away from her.

"Of course!" Raine couldn't keep the anguish out of her voice. He had arranged this seduction scene and she was playing her role exactly as he directed. "What woman could resist this highly romantic setting or a chance to make love to the famous Devlin Paige?" She got up on her knees, glaring down at him, her breasts heaving with agitation, and the coppery glow from the fire enhancing the agonized sparkle in her dark eyes.

Devlin questioned her startling change of mood only on one level. "Hey!" He got up on his knees to face her, grasping her by the wrists and pulling her back to him. "What the hell are you trying to do to me? What do you think this has all been about?"

Arching away from the violence in his eyes, Raine cried, "You arranged this setup hoping I'd do exactly what I foolishly did. Thank God I stopped myself in time. I won't be another female trophy to add to your collection. I don't want you that badly."

"What?" His fingers left her wrist to clamp around her upper arms, digging into the soft flesh. She had never seen him look more fierce.

His sherry eyes were hot, the grooves beside his lips deep with suppressed anger and frustration. "I won't let you spoil this, Raine," he bit out between his teeth. Her eyes were the wounded brown of a deer facing the barrel of a loaded shotgun, but he was without mercy. He jerked her to him, bent his head and crushed her lips beneath his. One of his hands came up behind her head and held it firmly in place while the kiss intensified. Defiantly she resisted him until she decided the best defense against him was a passive one and went limp in his arms. It took several moments before the lack of participation got through to him, but when it did he immediately broke off the kiss and let her go. His shoulders slumped and he sat back on his heels, staring at her with a bleak, defeated look in his eyes. "I didn't plan on it happening this way." Exasperation warred with the self-derision in his face. "I want you so much, I'll do almost anything to have you."

"And Devlin Paige always gets what he wants, doesn't he!" Raine spat out. "What I want doesn't come into it." She stood up quickly, reaching for her clothes. Clutching them into a tight wad, she started for the bathroom. Suddenly, even getting dressed in front of him seemed too intimate.

He blocked her way before she had moved more than a few feet. "What you want does come into it—you want me."

She read the steely determination in the rugged lines of his face, saw the stubborn angle to his chin, the steady penetration of his eyes and knew he would not be denied. His ego was so great, Raine thought, that he had no idea how self-centered he sounded. She raised her chin and glared up at him, trying to disguise how shattered she felt with as great a show of angry determination as he. "Wanting is not enough," she cried, her throat locked with pain as the tears began to roll down her cheeks.

"Damn it!" Devlin shouted furiously. "I'll marry you!"

"Why? So I'll have to go to bed with you?" she shouted back.

"Yes! If that's what it will take," he bellowed, then stopped and stared at her, a stunned look on his face. He raked his hand through his hair and looked upward as if he might find the right words written on the rafters. Raine's anger deflated as quickly as it had mounted. She took a deep breath and held it, waiting—knowing instinctively that they had just traveled in a direction neither of them had anticipated. She was paralyzed, unable to leave with his angry words hanging between them, yet wanting to run away, as far and as fast as she could. What kind of declaration had she just forced him to make?

When at last he spoke there was no anger, only a shattering remorse. "I never planned to say that." He shook his head, reaching out to grasp her gently by the shoulders. "Raine, you're driving my crazy. When I'm with you nothing goes the way it's supposed to. We should be making love, not screaming at each other."

He gave her a look of such naked longing that she felt her response from deep inside her body. "Is it love that you want from me, Devlin?"

"God, yes," he groaned, and folded her into his arms. His kiss was infinitely tender. He moved his lips over hers, tentatively asking for a response, his naked body telling her without words how much he wanted her. Loving him as she did, she could no longer deny her own responses. Her clothing slipped from her fingers as she melted into his embrace, hugging him tightly around the waist. When the gentle kiss ended, he whispered, "Can you love me, Raine?"

"Yes," she breathed, trembling with emotion. His face lit up with triumph and he swept her up into his arms.

"I'm not letting you go, Snow Maiden. I let you leave me once before and I'm not doing it again. We're getting married as soon as I can arrange it."

"Married?" she asked incredulously, her eyes expressing sheer joy. She did not question further but accepted his nonverbal answer from lips both exquisitely tender and warmly possessive.

As if she were supremely precious to him, he laid her back on the bed, worshiping her naked beauty with glowing eyes. Within seconds she was on fire with the same kind of longing reflected in his eyes, and she opened her arms, welcoming him into her embrace. Tenderness was replaced by a voracious hunger that consumed them both. They feasted on the manna of shared passion, stroking, caressing and drinking of each other as if they had both been starving. They were together at the zenith of desire and together when they plunged over the edge and flamed into one fire of exquisite sensation; they rose and fell from one level of feeling to the next, until they had mounted and savored them all. As the climactic shudders shook them, Raine grasped Devlin tighter, overcome by his power and drowning in the wonder of being his.

The low moan of the winter wind rising in the nighttime forest was the first sound Raine heard as her mind reclaimed possession and she opened her eyes, supremely content. Devlin was hers and she was his. The fire had bronzed the masculine length of his naked body, shadowed the angles of his face where it lay upon her breast. A smile played shyly on her passion-bruised lips and her fingers lovingly stroked the heated skin of his temple, awed by his lovemaking and thrilled that their coming together had been so beautiful.

She uttered a soft protest when he lifted his head, but he quickly stilled her by placing his finger over her lips. "We have hours and hours left to us, sweetheart. Nothing can touch us here."

And nothing did as they alternately talked and made love throughout the long star-silvered night. The last thing Raine recalled before falling asleep was Devlin murmuring, almost to himself, "I've told you more about myself than I've ever told anyone." He sounded as if he were surprised. Raine snuggled closer to him and closed her eyes, content with the knowledge that she was special.

Seven

"**W**hen we get back, I think it would be best if we didn't say anything about our plans to be married." Devlin's velvety, deep voice seemed coolly removed from passion as he and Raine made their way through the snow-covered woods toward the lodge. Raine was startled by his tone, which seemed to match the crisp air around them. So newly arrived to the magic of his lovemaking and the passions only he could arouse, Raine wanted to shout to the world, but he obviously didn't.

"Why not?" The short, suspicious question was out before she could think about it. Was he regretting last night's proposal in the bright light of day? Had he offered marriage only as a way to keep her with him through one long passionate night of pleasure in the highly romantic setting he had prearranged? She chastised herself: how could she have such doubts about him after all they had shared? But why did his answer sound so pat?

"I have a heavy concert schedule and there won't be time to get married before I leave on my final tour, and once it starts, I won't have time to spend with you. Besides, the press will get wind of this and hound us both night and day. I don't want you subjected to that, you're not used to it." He stopped abruptly and hauled her into his arms. "I don't want to share you with the world—not that one." His hold was fierce and possessive. Raine chided herself for having doubted him for even an instant. He brought a gloved thumb under her chin and forced her to look up at him. "No regrets this early, are there?"

"No... no," she denied emphatically, missing him already. "How long will this tour last?"

"My last appearance will be soon after the movie premiere. I'm sorry, but it was scheduled months ago. We can take a long honeymoon. You do understand why I think it best not to tell anyone about our plans?" His voice was gentler now, more like the one he had used in the cabin; and the soft smile that played at the corners of his mouth and eyes melted her earlier doubts. His gaze intensified as his eyes traveled from her eyes down to her mouth, where it lingered until with a low groan he brought his face closer and claimed her lips. His kiss was soft and loving as his lips gently crossed hers, then moved up to her eyes and forehead. He stepped back. "We'd better keep on moving or someone is going to come upon two frozen people locked in each other's arms deep in the north woods."

Raine giggled impishly up at him. "That wouldn't do for your image, Mr. Paige. You're reported to be one of the world's hottest lovers."

His smile fled immediately. "Can't you forget that image?"

Seeing the flicker of pain her jest had brought, Raine hastily admonished, "Oh, Devlin, I was kidding. You are far too sensitive." She tilted her head to one side and attempted to look coy. "You really are a hot lover, though."

His laugh emanated from the depths of his chest and resounded through the stillness of the winter morning. "What happened to my Snow Maiden?"

"She got thawed out, I guess," Raine answered, laughing with him.

"Not too thawed out, I hope. I plan to be the only one to keep you warm. For my own peace of mind, while I'm on tour, I just might lock you in a freezer." His voice was full of humor as he pulled her close to his side and they continued their walk through the heavy snow. The trail was packed and hard, but Raine still slipped in her inappropriate shoes. It was a bitter, cold morning and she shivered, moving closer to Devlin's warm bulk. Immediately he inquired if she was cold.

"Of course, you idiot! This gorgeous coat doesn't extend to my feet and these shoes weren't designed for trudging over ice-covered ground."

"No problem!" He swung her up in his arms and carried her easily. "Your feet weren't on my mind last night, or this morning. Too bad I had to let the horse go back to its stable.''

He carried her the remaining way to the lodge and didn't set her down until they were before the roaring fire in the main room. He plopped her down on one of the sofas and knelt down on the floor before her, removing her sodden shoes. ''Seems I'm always treating you for hypothermia.'' He glanced up at her with a thoroughly wicked grin. ''I liked the first time better, however. Then, I had your whole delicious body to work on.''

''Well, look who's here. We were about to send off search parties.'' Darryl's voice heralded his entrance into the room. Raine quickly attempted to pull her feet from Devlin's warm hands, her cheeks flushing; but Devlin held on, continuing his sensual massage.

''Good mornin', Darryl. Did you get enough shots for Raine's article? We've completed our interview—that is, unless you have more questions, Raine?''

Raine was grateful Darryl couldn't see Devlin's outrageous leer as his impersonal tone turned the conversation to the ostensible reason they had been invited to come. Fortunately, she had gathered enough material from the people at the party to make up for the lack of printable information gained from Devlin the night before; and she had the magazine's files to fall back on, if necessary.

"I'm going to do a series of articles," Raine stated impertinently, almost yelping when Devlin tickled the bottom of one foot.

"That was Pat's understanding all along." Devlin supplied the new information with a smug smile, eyeing Raine's look of astonishment with amusement. "This lady reporter has made quite an impression on all of us."

"That's great!" Darryl hooted. "Sheila will be ecstatic."

Raine could no longer hide the effect of Devlin's tapered fingers caressing her feet, and stood up from the couch. She excused herself to change clothes, leaving the two men discussing Darryl's plans for the layout. She crossed the room to hang up the beautiful fur Devlin had loaned her. The owner must have missed it and would be convinced it was stolen by now. She wondered to whom it belonged and intended to find out as soon as possible and apologize for having worn it. She mounted the stairs, taking one last look at Devlin before going upstairs.

Reaching the privacy of her room, Raine removed her dress and went to take a quick shower. She felt invigorated by the warm spray and returned to her room to pull on a pair of forest green wool slacks and a matching alpine sweater. Her feet were quickly covered with heavy wool socks and thrust into fur-lined ankle boots. She brushed her hair vigorously to put the waves back in order and applied a little makeup around her eyes to erase the evidence of her sleepless night.

When she arrived back downstairs, all but Gisela and Devlin were gathered in the dining room enjoying a hearty breakfast. Raine heaped her plate with scrambled eggs, Canadian bacon and a steaming popover fresh from the oven. She had just taken a seat next to Patricia when Devlin entered the room and gave her a broad smile. He went to the sideboard to fill up his plate and her eyes followed him. His hair was still damp and curling behind his ears from his recent shower. It took Raine a great deal of time to return her concentration to the food on her plate.

"I hope you enjoyed the party," Patricia said. "I lost track of you in the crowd. By the time everyone left it was too late for a re-hash."

"Don't worry about Raine, Miss Blake," Darryl interjected. "I'm sure she had a good time."

Raine nearly choked on her bacon and flashed Darryl a warning glance that would have withered stone. He took the hint and remained silent, concentrating on his breakfast, his lips quirking with suppressed amusement.

When Devlin brought his plate to the table and took a seat by Raine's side, Patricia asked, "How is the interview going? A number of articles on the movie will be of great help to us."

"My share is over," Devlin announced. "We should leave for Minneapolis later on tonight and I'll need to call Ron to go over some tour arrangements, but I'm sure I left Raine with enough information to keep her going for a while."

Only Raine and Devlin were aware of what kind of information he had imparted, and it was difficult to hide her reaction as Devlin lifted his eyes to her face and smiled. While she gave Patricia her thanks for agreeing to a series of articles about the movie, Devlin wolfed down his breakfast and went for seconds.

Jacob laughed at Devlin's robust appetite. "Looks like the outdoors agrees with you, Dev. I haven't seen you eat like that for a long time."

Raine's eyes stared firmly at her plate as Devlin quipped, "Fresh air heightens my appetite for a lot of things."

When the meal was over, Raine offered to help Patricia clear the table. All of the staff had been given the day off in recompense for having worked the entire night before. Devlin disappeared into the study to make his phone call to his agent while Raine and Patricia worked in the kitchen.

Raine volunteered to scrub the frying pans and Patricia gave her a grateful smile. "Hate those things," she admitted, but picked up a dishtowel.

"How did you like the coat?" Patricia asked as she dried a large skillet, looking more like a housewife than a glamorous star of the opera.

"Is it yours?" Raine asked with embarrassment. She knew she would have to explain why the expensive coat had been missing all night.

"Mine!" Patricia blurted. "I only wish it were." Seconds later, she gasped with chagrin. "My big mouth! I bet it was a surprise I've now totally ruined."

"What?" Raine was intrigued. "What surprise? Devlin didn't explain whose coat it was." Patricia's stricken look told her exactly whom the coat was supposed to belong to. "Mine?"

"Devlin brought it in to show me yesterday morning," Patricia admitted. "I thought he gave it to you last night."

"Well, he did and he didn't," Raine agreed mysteriously. She was done with the pans and quickly dried her hands. "I had better get to the bottom of this."

Raine went to the closet and pulled out the coat, unconsciously stroking the luxurious fur as she went to give a proper thank-you to its deliverer. There was no one in the hall outside the study and she could hear Devlin's one-sided conversation through the open door. She was about to walk in and wait for him to finish speaking to his agent, but his words stopped her.

"Why do you think I bought Raine the coat? Of course, I don't plan to marry her...."

Damn it, Ron! Will you listen to me for one minute?''

Raine wouldn't listen for another second! Those words were all she needed to hear. White-faced and sick, she whirled away from the door and ran to the stairs, mounting the steps two at a time and racing to her room. Once there, she thrust the offending sable away from her and stood staring at it as if it had turned into some kind of repulsive monster. Tears blurred her vision as she came to a decision. She went to the closet and began hauling down her luggage, ripping her clothes from their hangers and throwing them into her garment case. She cleared her personal things off the chest and threw them viciously on top of the wadded mound of clothing, then jammed the lid down on her suitcase and snapped the locks.

How could he have done this to her? How could he? Paying her off for services rendered like some kind of high-class call girl. Everything he had said had been a lie! No wonder he didn't want to announce their engagement— there was no engagement! Hadn't he admitted he'd do anything to get her into bed? He had said the evening hadn't gone as he had planned. She was sure now that a marriage proposal hadn't been part of his plan; but rather than let his perfect setting go to waste, he had offered to marry her. How many other women had he brought off with furs? Was the coat meant to replace the warmth she would lose when he discarded her?

She'd never trust him again! She knew she couldn't face him without making a hysterical fool of herself, and she wouldn't give him the satisfaction! She picked up a pen and scrawled a message on a piece of paper.

Sorry, I've changed my mind. Under the circumstances, I can't accept this. Thanks for the indepth interview. You've made my career.

She picked up the sable and the note and carried them to the next room, where she deposited them on Devlin's bed. Anxiously looking over her shoulder, she retraced her steps. It took only a few minutes to finish packing, pick up her luggage and dart back down the hall to Darryl's room. She knocked impatiently on the door and was grateful to hear his muttered call for entry.

Safely inside, she shuddered, dreading being bombarded with questions she did not have the composure to answer. Thankfully, after one look at her stricken face, Darryl behaved like the real friend he was. Twenty minutes later he had arranged for their departure without arousing suspicion, saying that he had to conduct some personal business in Bemidji. What the Retterings did not know was that Raine was accompanying him in the borrowed jeep. She felt like a fugitive as she escaped the lodge by the rear exit and climbed into the waiting getaway vehicle. She hoped Patricia would not think too badly of her when she wrote to her explaining as best she could her rude departure.

They left the jeep in town, arranged for it to be returned to the lodge and hired a car for the drive back to Minneapolis. Darryl seemed to understand that Raine didn't want to discuss what had happened. He tried to keep the conversation light; but when his remarks got no response, he drove in silence, leaving Raine alone with her bleak ponderings.

Throughout the long drive back to the city, Raine recalled all the lies Devlin had told her. Her mind was occupied with only one

thought—she hated Devlin Paige! As her unseeing eyes gazed out the window at the passing stands of pines, she began compiling ideas
for her article. Sifting through the information she had gathered about him, she embel-
lished the facts with her own knowledge of the
man. The legendary rock singer with the sensual power of a tiger knew exactly what kind
of weapon he had and ruthlessly used it to ex-
ploit women, both at his concerts and in his
personal life. Wasn't she a prime example?
The article took form in her mind and she took
great pleasure in devising subtle turns of
phrase to give the reader a thorough understanding of the man with the sexy mystique.
Darryl made no comment on the bitter twist to
her lips and she did not see his frequent
glances, for she was too busy venting her
emotions on an invisible piece of typing paper.

The next morning, the paper held real
words—the entire slanted article she had com-
piled on the ride home. She arrived at the office and promptly handed the completed
interview on Devlin to Sheila, along with another on the lovely party thrown by Patricia
Blake.

"Glad you're back early," Sheila greeted. "The deadline's been moved up. We want your articles in the next issue." The older woman scanned them both quickly, admitting that the party scene would be devoured by their readers, but was visibly astonished by the interview with Devlin. "This is certainly a unique approach. I may have to tone it down a bit." Shelia's brows rose. "Are you sure you want it printed like this?"

The rebellious thrust of Raine's chin was her answer. Sheila shook her head. "A pity. I thought you would discover that there was real depth to the man. I'll handle the photos along the line you suggested. That's an unexpected thrust to the story."

Raine lived in a state of expectant anxiety every hour after that. She was sure that Devlin's colossal ego would demand an explanation for her running out on him, but it seemed he didn't. Eventually, she accepted that her leave-taking had been a relief to him. He didn't even have to bother with the expense of presenting her with a coat. She had left without making a ripple—another insignificant scalp to add to his belt.

Raine's roommate, Connie Masters, didn't immediately notice the change in her friend. Connie was a flight attendant and her schedule kept her out of their shared apartment for days at a time. Raine had seen her twice since leaving the lodge and they had had only enough time to exchange some brief small talk. On weekends, when Connie was not on a flight, the two women usually enjoyed lengthy conversations about their various activities. Connie was as quick-witted as her sharp green eyes proclaimed and as bubbly as the riot of black curls on her head. When they finally had a few minutes to spend together, it took her seconds to see that something momentous had occurred with Raine since the last time they had talked.

In terrible need of someone to share her agony over Devlin, Raine told Connie the whole sorded story. True to form, Connie was instantly sympathetic and willing to do battle with the man who had wronged her best friend. "What a swine!" Connie placed a comforting arm around Raine's shaking shoulders. "Celebrities are the worst, babe. I ought to know. I wish you could have talked to me before going on that assignment. I've heard stories about famous men that would curl your hair.''

Although Connie was all sympathy, Raine could tell that she had been thunderstruck by hearing the name of Raine's betrayer. ''Went right to the top of the line, I'll say that for you,'' she murmured sardonically.

Connie didn't need to reinforce that theme, Raine thought miserably. She was well aware that there was only one Devlin Paige.

She knew it would be a long time before she got over him, but Raine tried to go on with her life as usual. When that didn't work, she buried herself in her work. She took the promotion the magazine gave her as an ironic benefit gained from Devlin's presence in her life. She didn't feel guilty about accepting the position in the features department. She knew that her stories on Patricia Blake and the cast of *Remember Yesterday* were good and that she was more than qualified, but it set her teeth on edge to think about the unjust means often employed to step up the journalistic ladder. Who you know, not what you know, was a firm maxim of life; and she had been naive to believe that she could have moved up as quickly on her own.

The series on the Retterings and the Paige article had been huge stepping stones; they had virtually guaranteed her a better job. She wondered if Devlin's reaction to her article would bring an immediate demotion back to the food department. She had no doubt that he would complain and complain loudly. Their conservative publisher might buckle beneath Devlin's censure and fire her. No, she chided herself, Sheila had given the interview her stamp of approval; so the only negatives would come from Devlin himself.

The entire office staff had been in an uproar when they received invitations to the Minneapolis premiere of *Remember Yesterday*. Raine had stuffed hers into the farthest recesses of her bottom desk drawer. She had read the early editions of her article on Devlin, which would be on the streets the morning after the local premiere, and was horrified at what she had written. Consumed with guilt, she had no intention of going to the opening, or to the reception afterward.

"Call on line three, Raine," the receptionist's voice came over the paging system.

Raine massaged the back of her neck and reached for the phone on her desk. She hoped the call was not another delay in her scheduled interview with the governor. She had discovered that none of the personalities she wished to interview were easily accessible and he had already rescheduled three times.

"Raine dear? It's Patricia." The contralto voice was the last Raine had been expecting to hear. She sat up straight in her chair.

"Patricia?" she inquired. "Patricia Rettering?" As if she could not believe her own ears, which had easily recognized the fabulous voice known to millions.

"Hope I'm not calling at a bad time, Raine, but I got your note and meant to answer it immediately. I have been most remiss, but I thought that since I'm in Minneapolis for the premiere, I'd call. Did you work everything out with your editor?"

Raine had almost forgotten the hasty excuse she had composed for her letter to Patricia. She had made it sound as if Sheila had demanded her back in Minneapolis immediately. She had explained that she hadn't had the time to make her proper goodbyes, as she had found out just as Darryl was about to pull out of the drive. It was a flimsy excuse and she was hotly ashamed of it. "All a misunderstanding, Patricia. I knew it wasn't like Sheila to issue orders like that, but it turned out that the deadline for my articles had been moved up so it was just as well I got back. I want to thank you for everything. You and your husband couldn't have been nicer to us."

"Devlin's not coming to the premiere," Patricia stated baldly, catapulting the conversation from the polite to the pointed in a matter of seconds.

"Oh," Raine hedged, "I'm afraid I may not make it, either."

"I know something happened between you and Dev." Patricia went right to the heart of the matter. "I can see that you will be no more forthcoming than he on the subject."

Raine took a deep breath and tried to compose herself. After all this time the mention of his name could send her pulses skipping like jumping beans let loose beneath her skin. "I'm sorry, Patricia," she finally managed to say in a voice that resembled her own.

"No more said," Patricia declared succinctly. Raine's instant relief left her unprepared for Patricia's next line. "I want you to come, Raine. If Dev isn't coming you have no excuse. I've told Sheila I won't take no for an answer and I do want to talk with you after the reception. I'm having a few friends up after the public affair is over.''

"I don't think that would be a good idea, Patricia,'' she stammered for an excuse, and finding none, blurted out the truth. ''When you read what I wrote about Devlin, you'll be sorry you were so kind. I'd feel like a rat accepting your hospitality when you are so close to him. I'm sorry.''

''I should have known you would think like that.'' Patricia didn't sound in the least upset. ''I may not agree with your viewpoint, but if you haven't slandered him, I'll have nothing to complain about. I'm sorry you went off without seeing him. I feel responsible. It was something to do with that damn coat, I know it. I should have never told you about it. Please come, Raine, if only to relieve my guilty conscience.''

Raine didn't know what to do. She couldn't have Patricia putting any blame on herself for what had happened between her and Devlin; yet she didn't want to explain what had really happened to anyone. She tried to put Patricia off, but true to her word she would not take no for an answer. Finally, with a long sigh of resignation, Raine agreed to come to the private party being held in Patricia's hotel suite after the premiere. She told Patricia she would sit in the press seats during the showing and meet the Rettering party after the public reception. She planned to skip the public event, feeling that she would probably be unable to face people immediately after hearing the music composed by the man she both loved and despised. Yes, she had admitted that she still loved Devlin, even after the callous way he had treated her. She might hate all he stood for and despise his cruelty, but she could not deny that her feelings for him were as strong and alive as ever. Her wanting him was a gnawing, powerful ache that would grip her like a vise, then leave her in a cold sweat of memories. His cold, calculating seduction haunted her.

When she replaced the receiver on its hook, she stared into space. How soon after she had filed that interview had she begun to regret her words? An hour? A day? She had even tried to change it, but it had already gone to press. She tried rationalizing her guilt by whipping herself back up into a fury; but at night the tender dreams of Devlin's lovemaking blotted her vengeance and softened her hatred, and the

guilt would return to haunt her. She might tell
the world that Devlin was only an attractive
graven image with clay feet, but what would it
take to make her believe it herself?

She didn't notice when Darryl came into her
office until he snapped his fingers in front of
her face.

"Have you read this?" He held out a celebrity tabloid and pointed to the picture on the
front page.

DEVLIN PAIGE ANNOUNCES RETIREMENT
AFTER DISMAL SHOWING AT LAST CONCERT

The bold headline captioned a picture of Devlin walking through a crowd of fans without
seeing them. His handsome face, devoid of all
emotion, seemed to leap off the page.

"You can't believe all you read," she managed. She didn't want anyone to believe one
word of her article, did she?

Quickly her eyes scanned the paper, narrowing as the condemning review went on to
describe Devlin's lack of energy on stage, the
disappointment of his audience and Devlin's
abrupt departure as soon as the concert had
ended. He had left his fans without one of his
traditional encores. Rumors were flying that he

was ill with some rare disease, that he might have burned out, that he had fallen in love with a woman who refused to share him with an audience—and they listed several possibilities. Raine cringed after each feminine name.

Raine found none of the excuses believable, and couldn't stop wondering about him. What was he doing? Where was he and with whom? The article said he had dropped out of sight immediately following his last concert. Patricia had told her that he did not plan to attend the premiere.

She took her purse off the hook on the wall by her desk and told Darryl she was going home. She had lost the ability to forget Devlin Paige by losing herself in her work.

Eight

The bittersweet music seemed to highlight the actors' every thought and echo the turns and twists of the plot. The characters came to life, Patricia Blake and Jacob Rettering parted by fame and brought together again by impending danger. Without departing from the purpose of accompaniment, the melodies wove in and out of the story and tied it all together, bringing tears when the characters ached with longing and joy when, at last, love came.

During that last surge of Devlin's powerfully orchestrated music, the credits rolled.

Raine quivered as she read: "Composed and arranged by Devlin Paige." She couldn't help the swell of pride that brought tears to her eyes.

When the lights came on and the screen blanked to white, not a sound came from the audience. Seconds later a loud thunder shook the frame of the theater as five hundred pairs of hands acclaimed all at once. *Remember Yesterday* would go on to be a triumphant success, a poignant love story made only more moving by the emotional melody that flowed like life's blood throughout.

Raine sat in her seat, unable to move. She had written that the composer of the most memorable theme she had ever heard was a craven image without depth. Tonight's performance proved to the world how supremely wrong one reporter could be.

As the crowd moved up the aisles to vacate the theater, she remained seated, listening to sounds she could no longer hear but could still feel in the depths of her heart—Devlin's music, beautiful and forlorn, joyous and sad. He had written notes for every emotion and they could all be heard, all be felt as the theme changed from one to another. Raine didn't

know how the others could leave so quickly
and go about their lives when hers had been so
irrevocably changed. Didn't they realize that
they had been witnesses to something little
short of genius? A modern-day composer who
could be subtle, yet powerful? A classical
movement that had been made real for today?
Had they listened to the music? Probably not.
Most likely they could describe each scene and
play back the dialogue, but how many of them
would recall the melodies that flowed
throughout? Perhaps a few. But that meant
only that Devlin had done his job well. His
music had provided a beautiful canvas created
by a master so the actors could move across it.

As if shaking off a paralysis, Raine got up
slowly from her seat. She gave the empty
screen a last look and walked up the carpeted
aisle. Once outside, she did not follow the
crowd, which was moving on to the hotel
where the producer, director and cast were accepting well-wishers and accolades.

Across the street from the theater was a
park. It was small and totally surrounded by
shops and traffic signs, but at least it had a few
benches where a person could breathe in the
cool spring air and dwell on her own thoughts

in private misery. Raine wore only a mohair shawl over her shoulders, but didn't feel the evening's chill or the coldness of the stone seep through the thin material of her skirt.

"Raine?" The feminine voice was familiar and Raine turned to find Evelyn Smythe smiling down at her. "I thought it was you."

"Hello, Evelyn. Did you see the film?"

Evelyn nodded, noticing the tears shimmering in Raine's brown eyes. "Love stories always make me cry, too. I guess it meant even more since I've known Pat and Jacob for so many years." All Raine could do was manage a brief shake of her head. "Want to tell me about it?" Evelyn sat down on the bench and faced straight ahead, letting Raine make the choice.

"I'm ashamed of the article I wrote on Devlin. It's going to hit the streets tomorrow. After hearing the music—I—I don't know what to do."

"Why?"

Raine turned to face Evelyn and couldn't help but react to the kindness she saw on Devlin's secretary's face. "I—I presented Devlin, using a beefcake centerfold format."

Evelyn grinned. "Why should that worry you? It should sell a lot of copies of this issue." She paused for a brief moment, before continuing, "I'm a little surprised, though. Your magazine doesn't usually do that kind of thing."

"My editor thought it was a unique approach," Raine stated contritely. "The interview makes him sound like a sexy piece of male fluff—a tasty bite for the female man-eaters of the world. Our photographer, Darryl, blew up a picture of Devlin wearing a pair of tight Levi's slung low on his hips. I don't know where he got it, but Devlin's nude from the waist up."

Raine would have said more, but Evelyn's explosion of laughter stopped her. How could the woman laugh? Didn't she know how damaging the article would be? Incredulous, Raine gaped, her eyes growing wider.

"Oh, honey, I think it's priceless. You'll probably help sell more of Devlin's records with that article than any other publicity that's been done on him. Dev has turned down offers for articles like that countless times. I'm sure he'll be furious, but he did grant that interview and that is the image that has made him a wealthy man. Believe me, he could use that kind of publicity right now. His concert tour still has one appearance to go—you heard that he walked out on the last one?'' Raine nodded, still speechless. Evelyn took her hand, still struggling with her laughter.

''Don't look so stricken. Devlin is retiring right after the tour, but he owes Bryer Records this last concert. Your article will insure that it'll be a total sellout. Women will show up in droves and it won't matter if Dev's got his heart in it or not.''

''There's nothing wrong with him, is there?'' Raine didn't care if his concert was a sellout or not. She cared about the man, even if he didn't care for her in return.

''All rumor and conjecture. He's just exhausted. He's been pushing himself too hard. He wants the tour to be behind him. You heard the kind of music he's capable of producing.'' Evelyn furrowed her brow. ''He should be alone in some quiet spot, writing—not on stage wiggling his backside for the benefit of a frenzied pack of fans. I sometimes can't hear him at all when he's into one of his numbers. He doesn't sing, he just shouts above the amplifiers.''

"He doesn't need a good voice," Raine agreed, and didn't notice the strange look Evelyn gave her.

They chatted companionably for a few more minutes, while Raine assimilated the information that her article would probably not harm Devlin's career but, rather, assist him. The public would accept her words at face value, but he would read between the lines and feel her contempt.

"Pat should be back at her hotel by now. Want to come with me to her party?" Evelyn interrupted her thoughts.

"I don't think I should." Raine stood up from the bench and shivered. "It was kind of Patricia to invite me, but I don't think I'm up to facing anyone right now."

"Oh, come on. A party is just what you need," Evelyn coaxed gently.

"I don't understand why she's so adamant that I attend." Raine was still hesitating. How could she spend the evening with Devlin's closest friends after writing such derogatory remarks about him?

"Pat thinks all love stories must have a happy ending, and she believes she threw a wrench into this one. I told her that Devlin probably messed everything up just fine on his own, but she wants to exonerate herself. Matchmakers like Pat have a strong sense of duty. She got it in her head that Dev cared for you and that's why she invited you to the party and to stay at her lodge. Now, she needs to hear that she wasn't responsible for the way things turned out between you and Devlin. I know it was more than business between you and Dev, but I guess not a true meeting of the minds, right?''

Raine started walking out of the park. "No, it wasn't a meeting of the minds,'' she agreed, her mind flashing sensual pictures of herself and Devlin naked and entwined before a burning fire. At least after talking with Evelyn she could face Patricia Blake without feeling an overwhelming sense of guilt. Evelyn would know what kind of publicity would be good for Devlin and what, bad. She had placed her seal of approval on Raine's article; so at least on one level, Raine didn't have to worry any longer. All she had to contend with was the knowledge that Devlin would despise her after the article came out—tomorrow morning.

Raine gave Evelyn a ride to the hotel in her car, and when they arrived a crowd of people was slowly dispersing through the lobby. "Looks like Pat has stopped giving statements to the press," Evelyn pronounced as she pressed the elevator button. They found the suite where only a few close friends of Patricia and Jacob were visiting together.

Raine recognized the director, Dean Farringer, and decided that the short, silver-haired woman with him must be his wife. The only actor from the cast of *Remember Yesterday* was Vivian Randolph, whose husband was the well-known personality from the Broadway stage, Jerome Maxwell. His tall, distinguished figure stood beside his wife, quietly chatting with the Farringers. Not intending to stay long, Raine draped her shawl over one arm. She was glad that she had worn a shimmering gold gown when she saw how formally the others were dressed. The soft fabric molded across her breasts and skimmed over her hips to fall in flattering folds slightly below her knees. The bodice was cut in a Grecian style, leaving one shoulder bare. Her hair was swept up into a knot atop her head, with many loose tendrils framing her face.

Patricia drew her into the sitting room; and when she would have liked to have hung back, Patricia put her arm around Raine's slender waist. "We're all friends here, Raine. Come join us for a drink."

Jacob was serving as bartender and placed a glass of champagne in her hand. The group took a few moments to toast the expected success of the film and give credit to the contributions of those in attendance. Raine was able to speak privately with Patricia when the others went to enjoy the panoramic view of the nighttime skyline offset by the floor-to-ceiling windows. "I want you to know that your telling me about Devlin's gift had nothing to do with my decision to end things between us. I discovered that it wouldn't work and I know now that my decision was the right one."

Patricia shook her head sadly. "I'm very sorry to hear that. I was hoping that . . . but it doesn't do anyone any good to go into what I was hoping." She glanced up and a pleased expression brightened her classic face. "Oh, my dear, I'm so glad you came."

Expecting to see another well-wisher, Raine smiled and turned around. The smile froze on her face. Devlin stood less than a foot away, devastating in black evening clothes and a white pleated shirt. He smiled affectionately at Patricia and bent down to give her a kiss on the cheek. The movement brought him even closer to Raine and as he straightened, his hand snaked out and clamped around Raine's waist. Unable to quell the bubble of panic, Raine backed away; but he tightened his grasp and effectively terminated her retreat with an intense look. Raine sensed the tight hold he had on his anger and knew that she had better not create a scene by trying to escape. Why hadn't she expected this to happen? There was every reason to suspect that Evelyn had accompanied her boss to the premiere. She should have guessed it was not merely chance that Evelyn had found her in the park and persuaded her to attend the party. Close friends were gathered here, and Raine couldn't convince herself that she was in that category with the Retterings.

Devlin sleekly thanked Patricia and ensured that Raine could not obey her instincts to bolt out the door by pulling her closely to his side. "Not this time," he whispered in her ear. His fingers moved around her side and dug into her skin as he guided her out into the hall.

He kept a tight grip on her as he pulled her down the softly lit hallway and paused before the door of another suite on the floor. Pulling the key from his pocket, he opened the door and pushed her through. He leaned against the door with his arms folded across his chest, barring any escape attempt she might have made. Raine felt a chill grip her spine as she read the cold rage reflected in his eyes that glared steadily at her. He stood silently, studying her as intently as she was studying him. She had longed to see him again, no matter how often she denied it. She let her eyes travel over him, remembering every line and plane of his face; but he glared at her with a fury that was so strong she felt suffocated.

Not able to withstand the force of his gaze any longer, Raine turned and took a few steps into the sitting room of the suite. Her knees were beginning to shake so badly that she sat down on the nearest piece of furniture. She clutched her purse and shawl to her breast and sat stiffly on a straight-backed chair pulled out from the desk. She riveted her attention on the view afforded by the large window at the end of the room, afraid to look at the man who stood sentry at the door. She sensed Devlin's advance across the thick, plush carpet. He paused to switch on one of the table lamps, then crossed the room to stand before the window with his back to her. His hands pushed back his evening jacket and rested on his hips, his legs apart in a defiant stance.

Raine sat mutely in the chair, her ankles crossed and her back rigidly straight. She wished she were curled up in the smallest ball possible in a corner of the large sofa nearby, but didn't dare move. The silence stretched between them and Raine found herself studying him, tangibly aware of every muscle beneath the smooth black fabric of his evening clothes. She could do nothing but wait for him to break the silence, fearing that anything she might say would anger him further. She pulled her gaze away from him and let it wander around the room, until she saw a copy of *Today's Woman* lying on the coffee table, opened to the glossy full-color centerfold of Devlin.

"Oh, my God," she breathed. An advance copy had been sent to him. No wonder he was furious with her. She had thought he was still angry because she had run out on him, and had hoped never to see him after he read that article. Now she was here, waiting like a prisoner for her execution. She continued to stare at the opened magazine as if it were a snake coiled and ready to strike.

Devlin didn't turn, but said, "I've read that damned interview, word by word! It would give me a great satisfaction to wring your neck right now!" His voice was low, each word spaced and backed by the contained rage he exuded.

Raine could feel a wash of embarrassed heat and then terrified cold flow over her body, as her numbed mind searched frantically for some response.

"Devlin . . . I can explain . . . I . . ."

"You can explain?" His voice was like a knife, slicing through the tension in the room as he spun around to look at her. "You're not the Snow Maiden I called you up in the woods—the Ice Queen is more like it! What an actress! I thought you knew me and I knew you. What a fool I was."

"Please, Devlin . . ." Raine felt every one of his words as if they were shards of ice cutting through her.

"Please, Devlin," he mimicked. "What would you have me do to please you, or have I already done it? I see you are no longer writing about vegetables, if you ever did," he sneered. "A night of passion in a cabin in the north woods was your ticket up the ladder, wasn't it?"

"No! That wasn't how it was! You must believe me!" she pleaded.

"Believe you? You won't fool me twice. You claim I'm shallow in that so-called in-depth interview. Am I supposed to be grateful for your damning appraisal of me?"

He advanced toward her and Raine felt too defenseless where she was. She shakily rose and rounded the chair, placing it as a barrier between them. Self-preservation came to the fore and her own hurt replaced her earlier fear. "My article describes exactly the Devlin Paige I met and interviewed. You proved to me all too well just what kind of man you are!"

"I haven't proved anything to you yet, lady," he snarled. "After that article do you have any idea what women are going to do at my next concert, or just on the street if I'm recognized?" He took off his jacket and untied his tie, slowly pulling the strand of black silk from under his collar and letting it drop on the floor. His eyes held her motionless. His fingers loosened the three buttons of his for-

mal vest and he shrugged out of it, letting it
fall to the floor. He stopped his advance and
unbuttoned his shirt, jerking it free from the
waistband of his pants.

Raine felt shattered as the crisp, pleated shirt
joined the other garments on the floor. She
gripped the back of the chair, her body poised
for flight. "What's the matter, Raine? Does
the sight of my bare chest frighten you? According to your own words, it's supposed to
excite you and you're supposed to throw
yourself into my arms. I'm making it easy for
you—you won't have to tear my clothes off,
yourself!" He struck the exact pose depicted
in her article, his thumbs hooked in the waistband of his pants as he lifted his foot and
placed it on the chair she had vacated.

Raine's eyes widened and she gripped the
only barrier separating them—the chair.
"What are you doing?" she moaned. Her eyes
were drawn to the silky line of hair that disappeared beneath his waistband. His humor-
less grin let her know that he had noticed the
path that her eyes had followed.

"I'm surprised you need ask that. According to you, women prefer me this way. You
have me all to yourself in a hotel room. What

an opportunity! What are you waiting for? I know your body is not as frigid as your heart."

"Stop it! I feel bad enough about that article." She edged toward the door, but before she had taken more than a few steps he was barring her way. He rested one hand on his hip, his stance nonchalant—as nonchalant as a waiting panther tensed to spring.

"You had time to change it if you'd wanted to." His words came out silkily, deceptively controlled. "You meant every word of it and still do, you conniving little witch."

"I . . . I tried, but it was too late!" Raine pleaded, but knew he would never believe her. It was time to retreat with as much dignity as possible. "I'm sorry, Devlin. I think it best if I leave."

The smoldering explosion she had been expecting came with a violent roar. "You walked out on me once, but this time *I'll* decide when you leave! According to you, women everywhere find my animallike aura irresistible. You are a woman, aren't you?" In a lightning move he pounced. Caught, she struggled against him; but he imprisoned her arms and lifted her off her feet and headed toward the bedroom. He kicked open the door and was across the room in two strides, throwing her on the bed and pinning her brutally beneath him. He pulled her hands above her head and held her chin tightly, forcing her head still. His mouth took ruthless ownership of hers, compelling her to accept his power and the bruising force of his kiss. She could feel every hard sinew of his body as his hips ground against her. Her moans of protest were lost as his free hand moved over her body, touching her in all the places that should have made her writhe with pleasure beneath him. Raine was powerless to stop him and remained rigid, feeling humiliated and demeaned by every movement and touch of his body.

His fingers burned a path beneath her skirt to the inner surface of her thighs, across her soft stomach and to the waistband of her panty hose. Raine cringed away from his touch. There was no sign of the tender, coaxing lover who had once held her in his arms. She shuddered and tears trickled down the corners of her eyes. "Don't do this," she begged.

Lifting his head, he seemed surprised to see her tears. "What's the matter, don't you like my moves?"

"Please, Devlin. You're hurting me."

His body went still. He stared down into her tear-streaked pale face, the anger dying in his eyes. "God, Raine. What you do to me," he groaned, releasing her wrists and using his hands to cradle her face—hands that were no longer rough, but tender. His eyes ignited to gold, staring at her bruised lips. He groaned—a wounded male sound deep in his throat. He lowered his head and soothed her swollen mouth with his, sliding his lips across its sensitive curves with light satin strokes.

Unprepared for the sudden change from violence to tenderness, Raine lay trembling. Feeling her shudder, he lifted his head to look at her, but she squeezed her eyes shut and turned her face away. Her action condemned him, cut like a knife through his heart; and a muscle jerked along his jaw. He took a long tortured breath and rolled off of her. He lay staring at the ceiling for several moments while Raine lay beside him willing her shaking body to relax. Then, he was up and striding through the bedroom door. She heard the clink of ice in a glass, and then there was silence.

More hurt than she could have believed possible, Raine got up from the bed and mechanically moved to the door. When she reached the sitting room, she saw him standing before the window, his back rigid. He held a bottle of liquor in one hand and a glass in the other. Mutely, she stared at his back, unable to think of anything to say that could lessen the trauma of the last few minutes.

She picked up her wrap and purse from where they had fallen on the floor and stood waiting, hesitant about leaving him and wishing there was some way to heal the breach between them.

"Get out of here, Raine," he said softly. "Get out of here and don't ever let me see you again. I can't take it."

The agonized strain in his voice drove her from the hotel room. She closed the thick door behind her and closed Devlin Paige out of her life. She staggered down the hall to the elevators, praying she wouldn't see anyone and that she wouldn't have to wait long. Once inside, she pressed the button for the lobby and slumped into a corner, grateful for the small velvet-upholstered seat there. She hugged herself in an attempt to quell her shaking limbs. She had had a narrow escape. She didn't know what had stopped him from venting his rage, but thank God he hadn't gone any further.

She ran her fingers through her hair, which had been loosened from its styled topknot and fell around her shoulders, attempting to put some order in it before the elevator doors opened to the lobby. She made her way to the parking garage and waited for the attendant to bring her car around. How she managed to drive home safely was a miracle, as tears blurred her vision and her thoughts were anywhere but on the traffic flowing around her. When she parked in front of her apartment building, she turned the car off and slumped over the steering wheel. She remained there until the chill evening air permeated her light wrap. She struggled to open the car door and shakily made her way into her apartment.

The apartment was dark and Raine didn't turn on any lights, letting the darkness cover her, shroud her in a protective blanket. She went into her bedroom and collapsed on her bed, fully clothed. She lay in the darkness, reliving every moment with Devlin. His anger was understandable, but a small spark of outrage began to flame inside her. After what he had done to her, didn't he deserve what she had written? His callous treatment had warranted every word! He had bought his way into her arms with false promises of commitment, then intended to pay her off with furs for services rendered.

But tonight there had been far more than anger and offended male pride in his words and actions. What was it? There had been a flicker of something else before he had advanced on her, stripping his clothes from his body like some call girl. Was it disappointment? Hurt? What had he been feeling when his anger had drained away and he began to kiss her with such tender kisses? She would never know because she never would see him again. He had savagely eradicated her from his life.

She heard the front door open and knew that Connie was home from her date and would want to talk to her. Raine slipped under the bedclothes and feigned sleep when Connie tiptoed past her door, pausing to look inside and passing on when she saw the seemingly slumbering figure. Raine lay awake the rest of the long night, shivering beneath the covers; but eventually her eyes closed and her mind shut off as the first streaks of dawn edged across the sky.

Nine

Raine's flight landed at Chicago's O'Hare Field over two hours late. She ran to the front of the terminal to hail a taxi to take her to the auditorium where Devlin's final concert was being held. Sheila had not realized when she sent Raine to cover the performance that she would have rather been sent to Outer Mongolia, but a good journalist did not turn down a prime assignment. Raine had made it her goal to become the best magazine journalist possible. Since Devlin had thrown her out of his hotel suite, Raine had lost all hope he would ever contact her, ever understand that she had loved him and wasn't capable of the kind of deception he had accused her of. Connie had tried her best to keep up Raine's spirits, but Raine sank into the depths of depression and functioned with some semblance of her normal self only at work. Even at the office, people made comments about the change in her appearance. Was she on a diet? Didn't she feel well? She tried to shrug off their questions and concentrate on her job, dashing off to interviews and typing late into the night. There were dark circles under her eyes and her slender figure now appeared fragile as a result of too many skipped meals.

During the taxi ride, she pulled out her compact and grimaced at the image reflected. She looked exactly like what she was—a harassed and frazzled traveler, late for an appointment and anxious to get there before she missed it altogether. She pulled a comb from her purse and dragged it through her mussed hair, touched up her makeup and smoothed the linen suit she wore, trying to erase some of the worst wrinkles.

When the taxi stopped in front of the concert hall, Raine quickly paid off the driver, giving him an unnecessarily large tip, then pushed through the heavy glass doors to the lobby. A blast of sound staggered her for a moment and she lost her concentration. The usher gave her a disapproving glance but pulled his flashlight out and held out his hand for her ticket. She followed him down the center aisle until they reached her row. She murmured embarrassed excuses to the people she had to climb over to reach her assigned seat. Her ears were aching as the amplifiers exploded with sound and the people in the auditorium screamed their approval. Finally she was able to take her first glimpse of the stage, and pain spread from her ears throughout her body.

Her eyes were glued to the central figure, drinking in the fluid sensuality of his body as he moved to the beat. He held a mike in his hand, growling into the sound equipment as he lifted one arm over his head to direct the backup band to follow him. The black pants he wore clung to every bone and muscle, emphasizing his slim hips and powerful thighs before disappearing into leather boots that began below his knees. His white shirt was open to the waist and his chest glistened with moisture. His auburn hair was damp and kept getting into his eyes as he twisted and turned on stage. He worked the lyrics to the song with his body until the audience roared, begging for more. Raine was held spellbound, aware, as every other woman in the audience was aware, that this man called out to some basic instinct dormant in each of them. She found that her palms were sweating and her lips were parted breathlessly as the sheer animal magnetism of Devlin Paige claimed her as a willing victim. She didn't have to understand the words he was singing—she understood every sensual suggestion of his lean, hard body. His energy captured every member of the audience and they waited for his unseeing glance to touch them, wished he was singing for them alone. When he completed the number and was down on both knees before them, holding the silver microphone as if it were a woman, the audience rose as one and screamed, calling his name and demanding more. It was the end of his first set and Raine saw him signal his band with his eyes; then he flashed the audience a rueful boyish grin and spoke into the mike. His voice was like a caress, a silky endearment that brought a collective feminine sigh from his fans. "I'll be back. Wait for me." He raised his arm and waved, then strode from the stage without looking back.

Raine couldn't get her erratic breathing back under control. Miserably, she acknowledged that Devlin had spoken to every woman in the room with the same sensual command he had once used with her. She had felt as if he had performed for her alone; but when the house-lights came on, she was aware there were thousands of other people inside the auditorium as caught up in Devlin's performance as she was. A teenaged girl sat next to her on one side and a matronly silver-haired woman on the other. The girl turned to Raine, her blue eyes sparkling in a pert, freckled face.

"Isn't he beautiful!" she breathed. "I could just die. I really could." Her dramatic statement brought an amused chuckled from the older woman.

"If I got a chance to be near him, death would be the farthest thing from my mind." She exchanged a conspiratorial look with Raine, and Raine found herself blushing.

"Imagine that," the woman declared. "A girl in this day and age who can still blush. I'm going out to see if I can get a glimpse of him before he comes back on stage. The bands usually get something to drink from the bar before they return to do their last set. Want to come?''

Raine shook her head. The last thing she wanted to do was take the chance that Devlin might see her. In the anonymity of the dark hall, Devlin couldn't make out any particular face. She could tell that the audience was important to him and wondered how he managed to come across as if he sang to each of them personally, when he could only feel their presence, but see nothing. She watched the teenager next to her join a group of giggling girls who were each glowing with ecstatic reaction to the concert. Strangely, she felt proud of every flowery compliment they bestowed on Devlin, smiled at their youthful reaction to his potent masculinity and understood completely why Devlin had a devoted following. She was under the spell he cast. His act was a purely primitive pleasure to be savored. It didn't matter that he shouted instead of sung, that he growled the lyrics instead of attempted to deliver them in a voice that could not possibly have been heard above the pagan beat of the drums and the amplified scream of electric guitars. He was more a dancer than a singer, his body feeling the words to his songs and becoming an integral part of the rhythm.

Behind the closed blue velvet drapes, Raine could hear the band tuning up for the next set. A blaring bass picked out a deep, pulsating exercise while a guitar shrieked, then died on key. The members of Devlin's band were all young and energetic. They were dressed in splashy shirts and a variety of tight pants, but not one of them had the presence or power of Devlin. When he came on stage, they faded into the background.

The audience hurried back to their seats as the houselights blinked on and off to signal the beginning of the second half. Raine leaned back in her seat and prepared herself for the onslaught of feeling that came over her again as soon as the curtains opened. Devlin had changed clothes during the intermission and was now wearing a black shirt with billowing sleeves and the same tight black pants.

His songs ranged from suggestive to savage, from nonsensical lyrics to guttural comments on society; but through them all came a jungle message as primitive as creation. Devlin Paige was a man—a virile man in his prime. At the end the audience was exhausted, breathing like thousands of runners who had gone the distance. Devlin was bathed in sweat as he agreed to a final encore. He disappeared off the stage and the audience began stamping their feet and shrieking for his return, unable to let him go. Raine waited with them, on the edge of her seat, frantically trying to catch a glimpse of his dark head where she could see movement backstage. She was hugging herself with both arms when Devlin walked out for the last time. He was wiping his forehead with a towel and carrying a wooden stool. He placed the stool in the very center of the stage and adjusted the microphone to his seated position.

"Bill, will you bring me my guitar?" He turned around to a man who was bringing the battered-looking instrument across the stage. Devlin took the guitar and ran his thumb over the strings. "Ready to indulge me?" he asked the audience, and they shouted yes with one voice. His smile was enough to get him anything he wanted.

Suddenly the stage went totally black; but an instant later, a single white spotlight shone on the solitary figure propped against the bare

wooden stool and lightly strumming a guitar
with long blunt fingers. A profound silence
permeated the auditorium, as if everyone inside the vast hall realized that they were about
to hear a totally different Devlin Paige.

"Perhaps you've heard that this is my last
concert," he spoke softly, but he had the total
attention of every person in the hall. "I'd like
to leave you with a song that says goodbye.
Every man has to accept the changes in his life
and I'm no different from other men. This
song was written for those who have discovered that dreams are fleeting."

Raine found herself staring at his face,
sensing she was about to hear something so
beautiful and painful she wouldn't be able to
bear it. His fingers began a melody and his
voice was rich and deep—low velvet tones that
shook her to her marrow, caressed every nerve
ending.

I loved a girl in the winter,
When our kisses froze white in the air,
When fire licked our icicle fingers,
She was there, she was there.

And she was. Raine closed her eyes and
could feel the glowing heat from the fire warm

her skin as she lay naked in Devlin's arms on the plush fur hearth rug.

She recalled waking to find herself in bed with a handsome stranger who grinned at her and made her love him as she would never love another. Devlin—only and always Devlin. Her mind called out to him, silently willing him to sense that she was still there and always would be; but his voice grew husky with emotion, empty with loss and more deeply melodious than Raine could have imagined. She heard every poignant word and remembered.

At the end of the song his voice trailed off to a whisper and the spotlight slowly faded to black until the vast auditorium was shrouded in shadow. When the houselights came up, the stage was empty. Devlin Paige was gone and with him he took Raine's soul, leaving her empty and overwhelmed with grief.

There was a stunned silence. No one moved or made a sound, as everyone tried to deal with his astonishment at Devlin's performance. The emotional ballad had been sung by a man with a beautiful rich voice—a memorable voice that only needed the accompaniment of a soft guitar to highlight its resonant quality. Raine lifted tear-drenched eyes to find that there was not a dry eye in the house. She floundered sideways out of the row of seats, which were still filled with people. As she fled up the aisle, the first sound of applause grew and swelled until it transcended everything else.

She hailed a taxi outside the concert hall and went straight to the airport, caught the next flight back to Minneapolis and was back at her apartment within four hours. Connie was away and Raine was glad to have the apartment to herself. She needed to be alone and dreaded the next day when she would have to return to *Today's Woman* with a finished article on the Devlin Paige concert. It took her all night to write the story. She had to throw countless sheets into the wastebasket, some wrinkled with the dampness of her tears. Finally, exhausted, and hollow-eyed, she had a two-page article that explained what kind of emotional havoc took place during a Paige concert. She wrote with her feelings, capturing a woman's response to Devlin and his music, ending with her reaction to the love ballad which was a total departure from the image that had made him a success. Her article was a tribute to a great talent and a message of love from a woman to a man.

The article was printed in the next issue and appeared under Raine's by-line. She could not look at it again and barely managed to accept the congratulations of her fellow journalists without breaking down. She told herself that all she had to do was take one day at a time. Someday the agony would have to soften, someday the grief would have to lessen; but every morning she woke up in the throes of a nightmare, only to discover that her lonely dream was a reality.

She threw herself into her work, hoping that while she was working on an assignment she wouldn't think about Devlin. But he was in her dreams at night, there when she read a newspaper or listened to the radio and heard a song he had written. Listening to his music was a need she could not escape. Although his new songs were sung by someone else, his voice came through. The music was full of melancholy, the words compellingly beautiful but sad. She wondered how he was able to produce such a wealth of new songs. Was he devoting himself single-mindedly to his work, as she was? Was he trying to forget? She couldn't allow herself to think that. He was reported to be working on another movie score and signed to compose the music for a Broadway production scheduled to open next year. He was far too busy to give even a passing thought to a woman he had known briefly last winter.

She visited her parents more often, finding the old familiar chores that had carried her safely through her childhood a means to forget.

She was helping her mother hang new drapes in the living room when they were interrupted by the sound of a car coming up the drive to their farmhouse. She offered to go see who was visiting and got down from her stepladder to look out the window. Her shocked gasp brought her parents on the run.

"Who is it, Raine?" Her mother leaned over her shoulder to look through the window. "My word! That isn't—it can't be... Patricia Blake?"

"Don't just stand there, Mother," John Morgan scolded, but his voice echoed her disbelief. Raine had told them about her meeting Patricia, but they had never expected to meet her themselves—certainly not in the old frame farmhouse they called home.

Raine's mind was racing. It had been more than two months since the first time she had met the Retterings. Two months since— "I'll get it." She shook off her memories and opened the door to admit their guests.

Jacob seemed even taller than she remembered, and Patricia, more beautiful. Raine introduced them to her parents, grateful that her father had managed to slip his feet back into his shoes to hide the outrageous striped purple socks that she had given him as a joke for his birthday, saying he dressed too conservatively. She wanted the Retterings to like her parents and she wanted her parents to feel comfortable in their home, even when they were being visited by such famous people. She shouldn't have worried, for after a few minutes the two couples were talking like old friends. Caroline Morgan bustled out to the kitchen to make refreshments and Jacob cornered Raine's father, demanding the whole story behind the stuffed elk's head that hung on the wall over the mantel.

"You never expected me to come calling, did you, my dear?" Patricia patted the camelback sofa and Raine came to sit by her side.

"I'm surprised," Raine admitted. "But it's a very nice surprise. My parents have always wanted to meet you. They listen to your records all the time and tune in to the Metropolitan Opera on the radio.'' She pointed to a huge wooden console that stood against the light oak-paneled wall of their cozy living room, furnished with family antiques.

"I'm glad I got the chance to meet them." Patricia glanced curiously around the room, smiling. "Your parents have a lovely home."

Raine agreed, wishing Patricia would hurry and explain her real reason for coming. She and Jacob hadn't driven all this way just to drop in and chat about furnishings and stuffed elks. Her pulse was hammering in her temples and her palms were damp. Had Patricia come to tell her that something terrible had happened to Devlin? No, she didn't act as if there were any tragedy to relate. Was this another matchmaking venture? Whatever it was, Raine could tell the woman was having difficulty coming around to explaining the purpose of her visit.

"How have you been, Raine?" Patricia's eyes probed Raine's face, making her feel that the question was more than the usual pleasantry.

"Fine. I've been very busy with my career."

"So I've noticed. That was an impressive article you wrote in the last issue of the magazine." There was a long pause, each woman silently gauging the other. It was Patricia who finally broke the silence with, "Well, aren't you even going to ask about him?" A smile played at the corners of her wide mouth.

"Of course—how is Devlin?" Raine stammered, wanting to know everything about him and trying not to show her reaction to the mention of his name.

"Covering up about as effectively as you," Patricia said bluntly. "You two are the most exasperating couple I've ever met! Each of you is dying to go to the other, but pride—or something equally ridiculous—is preventing you."

Raine's jaw dropped, ending up somewhere down by her ankles. "Patricia...I don't think you understand. Whatever was between Devlin and me is over. He doesn't ever want to see me again. He made that perfectly clear the last time we saw each other."

"In a pig's eye!" was the famous opera star's astounding rejoinder. "He was hurt by your estimation of him in that article. Don't you see what that indicates? If you didn't mean anything to him, he wouldn't have reacted like that. Others have written even worse things about him and he just laughed it off." Raine could feel a growing hope as Patricia continued. "Raine, I know you fairly well. You had your reasons for writing that article as you did. I would venture to guess that you were hurt about something and angry enough to embarrass Devlin publicly. What are you going to do, sit around and nurse your wounds for the rest of your life?"

Raine was saved from giving an answer when her mother came back into the room carrying a tray of thick sandwiches and a large pitcher of ice tea. "There's hot coffee, too, if anyone cares for it." She put the tray down on the large round coffee table and called to the men. "Come and have a sandwich. That hunting talk can wait until after lunch."

Able to put some order to her thoughts while everyone concentrated on the luncheon tray, Raine started a painful reevaluation of her past. Was she really allowing pride to keep her away from Devlin? Dare she take the chance that he would reject her again? More to the point, could her life be any more miserable if he did turn her away again? Did it really mat-

ter which one of them made the first overture
if there was anything left to salvage? The
practicality of seeing him soon was apparent
when she heard Patricia and Jacob mention
that Devlin was visiting them at the lodge.
Raine smiled for the first time in weeks as the
reason for the Rettering's four-hour drive became clear. As she listened to Patricia discuss
Devlin with her parents, she knew she would
be traveling back to the lodge with the Retterings.

"Well, princess, these people have traveled
a long way to get you." John Morgan's eyes
twinkled as he looked at his daughter. "Are
you going to make their trip a success?"

"I—I...yes!" Raine beamed at her father.
He had always known what she was thinking
before she revealed it aloud.

"Good." Jacob bit into his healthy sandwich as if the whole matter was settled to everyone's satisfaction.

Raine raced upstairs to begin throwing
things in a suitcase, but sat down halfway
through her packing. Her mother entered the
dainty pink bedroom that had been Raine's all
her life and sat down on the bed beside her and
pulled her into her arms. They exchanged

looks of complete understanding. "Oh, Mom, what if he doesn't want to see me?"

"You'll never know if you don't go to him, will you, darling?" Caroline helped her finish packing, and gave her a final hug and shoved her out the door of her room.

It took only a few more minutes to say goodbye to her father and apologize for cutting her visit short. She clung to her father's big frame like a little girl holding on to security. "Do you love him, honey?" he asked gruffly. She nodded. He grinned down at her. "Fallen in love with a rock singer. I was kind of hoping for a doctor, or maybe even a farmer..."

"He's a composer, Dad," she giggled. Moments later, Raine was seated in the back seat of the Retterings' Lincoln Continental, watching the passing newly greened countryside without registering much more than the knowledge that, with every passing mile, she was getting closer to Devlin. She tried to compose a speech, something wonderful and meaningful to begin their conversation; but her mind was a blank. She would have to operate from instinct, hold on to the hope that had risen like a tiny new bud inside her the moment she saw Patricia emerge from her car. She had needed this push to do exactly what she should have done immediately after the Chicago concert. She should have fought through the crowd and screamed at the top of her lungs, "I'm still here, my darling! I'm still here!"

She was willing to hang on for dear life to that tiny bit of hope—until she was either in the arms of the man she loved, or totally convinced that he would never love her in return. Patricia and Jacob had known Devlin for so long. They just couldn't be wrong about his feelings for her—they couldn't be.

Ten

Raine zipped up her lightweight jacket and jammed her cold hands into the pockets. The setting sun glowed red, the gathering dusk dropping a pale gauze curtain over the tender new leaves of the springtime forest. She trudged down the narrow muddy lane, her canvas shoes sinking into the thick layer of dried pine needles that covered the trail. With each step she took, she was that much closer to Devlin. Would he turn her away when she got to the cabin? The trail began a gentle decline and she quickened her step. This time, she would not be carried unconscious to the cabin by a handsome stranger, this time she would arrive under her own power and remain there until Devlin either told her he wanted her, loved her—or drove her away.

She was out of breath by the time she reached the base of the hill. When she had started out from the lodge, she had felt the evening dampness in every bone; but because of the brisk pace she was setting over the rough terrain, she was growing warm. She stopped to rest, staring through the shadowed birches and firs toward the rustic cabin where it had all begun. Devlin was there, preferring it to the lodge. Why, if he hated her, would he want to spend time at the cabin? That was a paradox, unless... Doubts coursed through her, whittling away at her confidence. He had come to the cabin before to relax. He could be doing just that now—if she meant nothing to him. She saw a thin column of wood smoke rise from the cabin's stone chimney and her heart began to flutter. In a matter of minutes she would see him again and her questions would be answered.

She began to cross the clearing but stopped after a few yards. Several wisps of tawny gold hair had escaped from beneath her cap, and she quickly tucked them back. Her heart was in her throat by the time she had gathered enough courage to walk up to the door. Devlin's voice stopped her before she could knock. He was playing the guitar and singing in the beautiful melodic voice she had heard at his final performance. She carefully pressed her ear to the door. Words drifted through the slatted wood, but then the deep guitar reverberate with a discordant twang, and then there was silence. She stepped away from the door, staring at the frozen ground beneath her feet. There had been a lonely quality to the song that expressed what she had been feeling for weeks but had never thought to put to words.

Was this song written to bring an audience to its emotional knees, or was it possible he was interpreting his own feelings, from his heart?

Patricia and Jacob had convinced her that Devlin loved her. During the hours in the car as they traveled north, Raine's confidence had grown. She had to take this final step. She had to tell Devlin how she felt. Summoning all her courage, she knocked on the door.

No movement could be heard from inside, and she feared he might not answer. She knocked louder, bruising the knuckles of her hand, and heard his smothered oath, then angry footsteps as he came to the door. He pulled it open and, abruptly, they stood face to face. All of her well-thought-out speeches fled her mind when she read the frigid rejection in his eyes. There was no flicker of pleasure to be seen in the chiseled features, no softening in the strong jaw. Her eyes dropped to the ground, unable to withstand his frozen stare. In a daze she saw that his feet were bare, and she said the first stupid thing that came into her head. "You'll catch cold." She sensed his withdrawal and her heart sank. "May I come in?"

"If you must." He backed away from the door and she walked inside. She stood staring at the opposite wall as he closed the door behind them to shut out the brisk evening air. Raine knew that she would probably be better off outside, for the temperature inside the cabin was steadily dropping as his silence grew painfully longer. Where was the response she was supposed to have seen when he first looked at her? Could he stare at a woman he loved without showing any sign of pleasure? She was positive that her own face had registered her longing, but his had reflected no tenderness at all.

"What do you want?" he asked warily, not moving from his stance by the door.

"I...I wanted to see...I wanted to talk to you about..." She was stammering as she turned to face him, backing down from the coldness in his expression.

"Don't tell me," he jeered. "Pat sent you. Has she filled your head with some farfetched tale that you would find me languishing away? I assure you I'm not. I came here for a little privacy." He waved his arm to point out the cluttered condition of the cabin. "I've been too busy to clean, so I won't offer you a chair. Unless you have something more you wish to say to me, I think you should leave." He stepped to one side, making it clear that he expected her to go.

She cleared her throat. "It...it was a long walk and I'm cold. Would you let me have something hot to drink before I leave?" She was pleading, stalling for time, and she knew it. She had known it wouldn't be easy, but his ice-cold reception had knocked the props from under her feet and she wasn't sure how to proceed. Maybe Patricia and Jacob were wrong. "A cup of coffee?" She offered the suggestion hesitantly, hoping it was not too much to ask of him when he obviously couldn't wait to see the back of her.

She squirmed miserably through another long pause. "The pot's empty, more'll have to be made." He was terse and his words almost bordered on rudeness, but she was too unhappy to care.

"I'll do it." She moved to the kitchen area. "I don't want to put you to any trouble."

She thought she heard him mutter something under his breath, but she couldn't be sure and didn't dare ask. She pumped water into the blue spattered-enamel coffee pot and carefully measured the grounds before placing it on the stove to heat. It seemed rather foolish to keep on her jacket; so she took it off and hung it on a peg on the wall. She pulled her cap from her head, brushing the golden curls from her face as she perched the cap on top of her jacket. She didn't know what to do with herself while she waited; so she pushed her hands into the front pockets of her brown cords and stood staring at the coffee pot waiting for it to perk. She didn't realize that her shirt had come loose until she noticed her shirttail dangling below her forest green crew-necked sweater. Hastily she began tucking her shirt back in, and it was then that she got the most peculiar sensation. She glanced across the room and found Devlin staring at her, his hazel eyes intimately assessing her figure.

She sucked in her breath sharply, her whole body vibrating with elation. He wasn't unmoved by her presence—he felt something. She recognized that look and took courage.

She returned his assessment, unable to stop herself. Slowly her eyes moved down his throat to the deep vee of his sweater. She saw the curling, darkly bronzed hair that she knew covered his broad chest. The muscles of his shoulders rippled the soft knit, as her melting glance moved down to his waist and over the light denim stretched across his slim hips. Her lips parted unconsciously and her temples began pounding as warmth spread inside her.

Her nipples sprang to life beneath her shirt and without thought she placed a hand on her chest to calm herself. The action seemed to ignite a fire in his eyes and he began moving toward her. ''It's always the same between us, isn't it?" His voice was husky with strain. He continued to approach and she stared, stupefied, straight into his deep hazel eyes.

"What do you want from me, Raine?" he groaned as he pushed her hand away and placed his own where hers had been. "Is this what you came for?" His thumbs brushed over her nipples and she closed her eyes for a brief moment. His face looked strange, a knowing expression darkening his eyes, as if he enjoyed proving she had no way to hide her response to him. She couldn't answer and he lifted her breasts from beneath, gently pressing down on her tingling nipples with his forefinger. They were both breathing hard; but unlike her, he had the power of speech. "Why should I give you anything, Raine? All you've ever done since we've met is taken."

At last he was letting down some barriers, asking questions that she wanted to answer, had planned to answer since the first moment. Unfortunately, she was incapable of forming a verbal response, her whole being centered on the caressing fingers that had taken possession of her. She swayed toward him and instantly his hands dropped away. "No," he gritted. "I told you once that I never wanted to see you again and I meant it. That time, I almost took you by force. Do you know what it does to a man to realize he is capable of that kind of violence?''

The self-disgust in his voice restored her swimming senses and she regained her power of speech. ''But you didn't, Devlin. You were hurt and angry, but you didn't hurt me that way.'' She flung herself against him, wrapping her arms around his chest and refusing to let go.

He froze. ''God!'' he cried. ''Are you trying to drive me completely out of my mind? I can't be near you without wanting you. Get out of here, Raine, while you still can.''

''I love you,'' she said desperately into the soft cashmere of his sweater. Terribly afraid he would force her away from him, she began to cry. She clung to him with all her strength when his hands came down on her shoulders and he tried to push her away. Suddenly her words seemed to penetrate, for he shuddered and stood perfectly still. He placed his hand under her chin and made her look at him.

''Say that again.'' Sherry eyes probed her brown ones, flickering like multifaceted jewels, then flaming to gold-flecked brandy as she repeated her words. "Then why? Why have you put us both through hell? Why did you run away from me?"

When she didn't answer immediately, his thumb pushed incessantly on her chin and he demanded, "Why, Raine?"

"I heard you talking with Ron that day in the lodge. You... you said you didn't plan to marry me. Patricia had just told me that the fur coat was a present you planned to give me. You told Ron... that you bought the coat to... to..."

"You thought I planned to pay you off with a fur for letting me make love to you?" His voice was thick with disgust. He dropped his hands away from her and raked one of them through his hair. "My God, Raine, I asked you to marry me."

"You never asked. You said you'd do anything to get me in bed. I forced you to bring up marriage. You even said you hadn't planned on saying anything like that."

"What?" He was thunderstruck, finding it incredible that she could have so misunderstood him. "I told you I loved you that night, over and over again."

It was her turn to look incredulous. "Not once did you say those three words to me."

His voice rose. "Dammit! My whole body said it! Why do you need the words?"

Her voice matched his. "You needed them from me!"

"And you never said them until today!"

Sparring eyes clashed until the significance of what they had just said to each other became clear to them both. They stood gaping, until Devlin's face split in a sheepish grin. "It's happening again. Every time I try to explain how I feel about you, we end up shouting at each other. Let's make a deal. I talk first and you don't open your beautiful little mouth." Unable to suppress an answering smile, Raine agreed and went willingly as he pulled her along and firmly pushed her into the rocking chair. It was not the same one that used to be here, Raine noted. This one was not a prop, but a genuine antique, its arms worn and smoothed with wear. Devlin dropped down into an opposite chair. Everything had to be real this time—everything.

Devlin started to speak. "I wanted everything to be perfect when I proposed to the woman I loved." He gave her a pointed look, which she accepted with a gracious nod. "Now, how was a famous rock singer supposed to impress his lady love when she already expressed open contempt for his image? Go all out, I figured. So I planned the whole thing out. I spent hours unpacking crates until the cabin was furnished exactly right. The fire was burning, champagne chilling, and I arranged for a romantic sleigh ride in the snow. I bought a beautiful coat to give her. Oh, Raine," he blurted, "I wanted to see you wrapped in fur, wanted to know that it would keep you warm when I wasn't there to hold you in my arms. If you had just once put your hand in the pocket of that coat you came to despise, you would have found your engagement ring. I thought it would be a special way of giving it to you."

Unable to remain quiet after this startling revelation, Raine exclaimed, joyous tears shimmering in her eyes, "Oh, Devlin. I . . . I thought I was just another girl to you. I couldn't trust you and couldn't believe that I was special to you. How could you love someone like me? Every woman in the world is in love with you and I was just one among millions."

"You are one in a million, Raine Morgan," he corrected her, then stood up and crossed to her chair, pulling her up out of it by both hands. "I've adored every inch of you from the beginning."

"Then why did you want to keep our relationship a secret?" She leaned into him, laying her head against his shoulder, breathing in his familiar scent, hearing his heart beating beneath her cheek.

He wrapped his arms possessively around her and pulled her with him as he sat down. Settling her on his lap, he explained. "I wanted to protect you from all the publicity I knew would come the instant our announcement was made. You would have hated it and I was afraid you might resent me for subjecting you to it. Besides, you are too precious for me to want to share you with the world. I knew that on tour we would only have had a few minutes together, but that after my final concert you and I would have time to be alone and not be hassled by the press." He grinned down at her. "My image days are over, sweetheart. The public's not as interested in composers as they are in performers."

"Oh, Devlin, I love you so much that I would have taken those few minutes on tour and cherished them. I was in Chicago and heard you sing 'Girl in the Winter.' It was beautiful, but I was sure I had lost you forever."

"You'll never lose me," he declared. "I should have put that ring on your finger to remind you that you were mine forever." He pushed her head against his chest and smoothed her hair with his hand. "I just plain forgot about it after we got to the cabin. The ring wasn't as important as talking to you, loving you."

He took a deep breath, and leaned his cheek on the top of her head and linked his hands behind her. "Your little note destroyed me. I thought you had found the ring and didn't want it. That's when I decided that you had let me make love to you as payment for the article you planned to write. After reading it, I was convinced that you were after that interview from the beginning. I guess I didn't trust you any more than you trusted me."

Raine wrapped her arms around his waist, tightly. He was as vulnerable as she. He continued to explain things, but all she really cared about was his love for her. He had loved her then and he loved her now, even after the mess they had made of their lives.

"What you heard me telling Ron that day was that I didn't plan to marry you until after my tour was over. He was putting up quite an argument about my quitting performing, and seemed to think I was ready to drop all the concert commitments when I told him I was going to marry you. If you had listened a little longer you would have understood what I was trying to tell him—you do believe me, don't you?"

"Yes, and I'm more sorry than you could ever know that I doubted you and ran."

"I'll never let you get away from me again," he promised thickly, and framed her face in his hands. His lips dropped to hers, gently brushing across her mouth until she melted against him. His kiss deepened as his mouth hungrily devoured her softly parted lips. Raine couldn't get close enough to him. She wrapped her arms around his neck, letting her fingers spread through his hair and hold his head. Happiness greater than any she had ever known burst like a myriad of shining light inside her as his lips caressed every inch of her face, gently brushed away her tears and returned to her mouth.

Devlin's large hands released her face and traveled down her body, molding every curve. His fingers fumbled beneath her sweater, tugged at her skirt, then slid over her soft skin to her breasts. Raine was just as eager to touch him, her hands slipping under his sweater and pressing against the curling hair that hazed across his chest. "I can't get close enough to you," he murmured against her lips, then swiftly stood up with her in his arms and started toward the bed. He dropped her on the soft mattress and stood over her, roguishly grinning down at her. She reached her arms up to pull him down to her, but he hesitated then turned to walk across the cabin.

Raine was so confused by his action that she remained on the bed, watching him rummage through a rucksack by the door. He retraced his steps to the bed, with one hand held tightly closed. "This time," he began as he came down beside her, "there'll be no misunderstandings. Hold out your hand."

Raine held out her left hand and watched through misting eyes as he slipped a ring on her finger. A smoky topaz surrounded by diamonds flashed in the dim light before Devlin lowered his lips and kissed the ring on her finger. "This ring reminds me of the warmth in your eyes." He looked up at her. "I'm tired of carrying it around—the answer I see there is yes, isn't it?"

"Oh, yes!" She wrapped her arms around him and gloried in the feel of his arms around her, knowing the golden stone on her finger would always remind her of the gold flecks in his eyes.

"My time alone has ended, Raine," he whispered huskily. "My winter lady is here where she belongs."

* * * * *